The True Story of
Mary Bryant
Escape
FROM BOTANY BAY

GERALD & LORETTA HAUSMAN

ORCHARD BOOKS • NEW YORK • AN IMPRINT OF SCHOLASTIC INC.

For Mary in the light
— G. & L. H.

Sources

Research on *Escape from Botany Bay* was greatly helped by the following five books:

A First Fleet Family, by Louis Becke and Walter Jeffery (London: McMillan & Co., 1896).

Boswell and the Girl from Botany Bay, by Frederick A. Pottle (London: William Heinemann, 1938).

The Strange Case of Mary Bryant, by Geoffrey Rawson (New York: E. P. Dutton, 1939).

Botany Bay, by Charles Nordhoff and James Norman Hall (New York: Sundial Press, 1944).

To Brave Every Danger, by Judith Cook (London: Macmillan London Ltd., 1993).

LIBRARY OF CONGRESS CATALOGING-IN-PUBLICATION DATA AVAILABLE.
ISBN 0-439-40327-8

10 9 8 7 6 5 4 3 2 1   03 04 05 06 07
Printed in the U.S.A.   37
First edition, April 2003

Mary Broad Bryant was an eighteenth-century teenager whose theft of a bonnet sent her to jail in Plymouth, England. There her story might have ended, but she was transported to New Holland as part of the First Fleet. This was England's way of colonizing the country that would become Australia — with dying prisoners, forced labor, and insufferable conditions.

Amazingly, Mary survived it all, and her saga of Botany Bay and her escape of three thousand miles in an open boat with husband, two children, and seven other convicts is the stuff that movies are made of. Even in her day, the Mary Bryant story, as it were, reached a large number of readers through the earliest London broadsheets, precursor to our present-day newspapers.

Mary was the most famous survivor of her time. More surprisingly, her open-boat voyage has never been bested by a woman. In her day it was done by Captain Bligh, but he was a seasoned navigator whereas Mary was an unskilled woman who knew more about skinning pilchards than raising sails.

What drew us to Mary and her unbelievable voyage was not just her great courage and undefiled spirit. We saw in Mary and her world a paradigm for many of the ills that plague our present society.

Mary, however, was not about to be silenced — not by time, history, or any other thing.

Her words ring true. Although she was illiterate, she spoke to the famous lawyer James Boswell, who defended her in an eloquent fashion. The record of Mary's trial — and trials — on this earth are found in journals, histories, and interviews. We studied all of them, and this book grew out of our admiration for this plucky, impassioned humanist who, for the past fifty years, has remained largely unknown.

By casting Mary's spoken tale in the first person, as if she were reeling it off to James Boswell, as in fact she did, we sought to recapture the immediacy of Mary's plight. To the extent that we succeeded, we may thank her. For, many times, we felt her presence. "Say it this way," we imagined. "No, don't say it that way; I never would've said that."

Writers of biographies often swear they see the stalking figure of their obsession as a ghost looming in the shadows. In our case, Mary Bryant was always bravely in the light, not where we could see her but where we would hear her, loud and clear.

GERALD & LORETTA HAUSMAN

The Theft

January 1786

⛵ I always wondered why the unjust went unprosecuted. When I was but nineteen years of age, I'd seen my share of executions. Not one, I can tell you, was a person of means. All were, without exception, poor people, like myself.

Consider, if you will, that the cost of a candle in Cornwall was too great to bear. The common salt with which we cured our pilchards was also too dear. Wet summers, bad harvests, high taxes, and the theft of our land by the privileged drove many an honest man and woman to thievery.

I myself looked hunger in the face and decided that, as there was no need for food on the gallows, I would throw my lot in with those who stole to stay alive.

They said I was comely, tall for a Cornish girl, with long dark hair and gray eyes. My face was clear and without scars or pox. You might ask why I couldn't find employment as a barmaid or as a servant. Well, I tried both with little success. The wages wouldn't support a cat, let alone a family of four.

My sister Dolly worked at Solcombe as a ladies maid. Solcombe was an estate way off on the Isle of Wight. I saw her petty wages often enough and supplemented them by snaring a rabbit or two from the local crofts. One day Dolly brought home a silver spoon wrapped in a silk handkerchief. This crime wasn't the same as treason, mutiny, or murder. Yet, believe it or not, a spoon and a handkerchief would see you swinging.

I knew a man who stole a lemon. John Tout, by name. He rotted, billeted to a post, on the road to Bodmin Gaol. Carrion's meat is the end of many a thief. But better to be killed, I say, than to shiver your life away in the dank, dark gaol. Imagine a four-foot-high cell, the only light coming through a slit in the wall. And the rats!

Well, I made my decision to come quickly to a good, or a bad, end. We Cornwall folk were always a bit mad and given to our own ways. We never saw anything wrong in taking what we needed thereby to live. For hundreds of years we slipped the noose, plying the smuggler's trade as we saw fit.

Thus I took to the woods and became a highway woman.

I knew enough of woodland ways to survive in the fresh air of Fowey. My accomplices were Catherine Fryer and Mary Haydon, both of them friends from days of old.

So, this is how we did our secret and dangerous deed. This is my story as I have remembered it: a true tale, spoken not written by me, as you will understand that I had no schooling, and wanted none.

Of a midnight clear we girls waited for a farmer's cart. Catherine and Mary Haydon pretended to be in distress. So, the cart stopped. Then, from behind a tree, came I, and with no weapon other than a paring knife, held the driver at bay. Meanwhile, my companions searched the man and his cart for anything of value.

If you think me wearing full skirt and bodice, you're wrong, for I'd dressed in breeches and a leather gherkin. I'd tied my hair back like a man's and over this I wore a floppy hat.

Did I look like a woman?

Not hardly.

So, as I say, we did the robbery as clean as clean could be. Then, instead of taking to the woods, we headed for high headland hills of slippery granite. And went down to the sea, and hid in a cave. There, as the breakers smote the limestone ledges, we counted coin.

I must say, this first theft was a bit too easy . . . and what a paltry take, too.

For some time after, we lay low. Make no mistake, though: My portion of the robbery appeared in a covered breadbasket at my mother's door. My father was upon the sea and wouldn't return for some time yet, which left Mother, Dolly, and me at wit's end for food. But now, Mother would be taken care of. I, for my part, ate cockles, mussels, and limpets scraped from the rocks. In addition, we had the odd, snared rabbit, and the occasional dove brought down by a stone.

Our wood's house was made of sod and covered over with leaves. We excavated the side of a small hill and took our comfort as we could. The natural cave where we'd counted our booty was too cold to live in. Nor was it as secure as the woodland retreat. We had one blanket and a worn-out robe between the three of us. Fire, we knew naught, unless in the foggy nights. Then no one could see the flames and we cooked little wood pigeons over charcoal, which gave no smoke but some warmth.

The damp cold, I want to tell you, would've made me into an old crone before my time. But fate had a different plan. Our highway efforts ended before they could scarce begin.

One sunny morn, I told Catherine and Mary Haydon, "If we continue this way, we'll surely starve."

"Or worse," Catherine muttered.

"What I wouldn't give for a hot cup of tea," said Mary Haydon, coughing.

"Who among us hasn't lice and fleas?" I asked.

Bent and cold, we shivered in the weak sun.

"Tonight, then," I told them.

Catherine wiped the soot from her face.

"Come hell, or high tide, we'll hold someone up who has the means to provide!"

"It's that, or wither up like summer snails," cried Mary Haydon.

Silently, we three nodded and, putting our hands together, avowed to rob a rich person on the road that very night.

The moon proved thin and the fog thick as bunting come

nightfall. We journeyed through the dewy grass to Plymouth, where we held up a woman on the main road to Plymouth Dock.

There our fate was sealed.

For the high-toned woman we robbed put up a terrible fight. Rather than serving up her purse, she struck us repeatedly with her walking stick. Worse, she began to scream. Catherine took a blow to the skull and fell all in a heap, at our would-be victim's feet. Then, Mary Haydon stepped in quick and pinned the lady's arms while I pummeled her with my fists.

Down she went on top of Catherine, who was just waking up.

I grabbed the lady's silk bonnet and her purse.

Mary Haydon got Catherine to her feet. We struggled off into the Plymouth fog. However, in our confusion, we went straight into town rather than off to our woodland hiding place. The moment I felt my feet striking cobbles instead of soft leaves, I knew that all was lost. We were quickly captured by townspeople, who heard our lady's screams. So for the sake of a silk bonnet and a few shillings, we were gaoled. Over and over in my head, my chains clinking at my feet, I heard the judge's iron decree.

"Hanged by the neck until dead."

And although he added, "May God have mercy on your soul," I knew he didn't mean a word of it.

The Prison

March 1786

Night after night in Exeter Castle, I wondered at what might be my fate. Would I go to the gallows in my soiled and ragged clothes? Would the crowd of onlookers cheer, or scold? Would the hangman, though masked, be someone who once knew me? Most dreadful, would my disgraced parents, William and Grace, be somewhere at the very back of the rabble, hiding their faces in sorrow?

I must confess, I had no hope.

My life seemed no more, and no less, than the dirty straw I slept upon. My sentence was set for the end of March, but some days before, a gaoler called my name. He was a gap-toothed, coal-eyed man, and he pressed his face to my cell door.

"Mary Broad, is that you?"

Rousing, I raised my head. However, I could not get up, as there were irons at my ankles, with a chain attached to an iron belt at my waist. Walking was difficult; so was standing. I found it best to sit. I'd not fully learned to trust my feet with these heavy irons. Besides, I knew, or thought I did, what he was going to say.

Forthwith, I looked him full in the eye. "If it's bad news you bring, get on with it."

He rolled his eyes and stroked his blue-stubbled chin.

"'Twas not in the orders that one so pretty was under my care." He dropped his eyes and shook his head solemnly. He meant me no harm, I could see that.

"Be of good cheer, Mary," he said softly.

I felt my heart begin to pound.

"On what news?" I murmured.

"Well, first off, you're not to hang. Your sentence's been commuted to seven years' transportation. Do you know what that is, Mary?"

In the adjoining cells there came the ringing of chains, which could only mean that Catherine and Mary Haydon were getting to their feet.

"What's transportation?" Catherine asked.

Mary Haydon asked, "Are we to get the same?"

"Hold on, ladies. One at a time," said the gaoler.

I tried to stand, using the cold stone against my back to steady myself. My head started to swim.

When next I spoke, my voice quavered.

"Am I not to die before I reach twenty?"

"You're all going to be transported, Mary. You and your friends are going to leave England for seven long years. But you'll live to see your twentieth."

The gaoler then wheeled around. He walked potbellied down the dark corridor, and disappeared.

I stood up and turned around. The chain that connected my shackled feet to the iron belt at my waist was heavy, but I was still able to draw my face up to the window slit.

"We are free, then!" I said.

Catherine and Mary Haydon were too stunned to speak.

When my hard crust of bread, my bit of cheese, and the sour small beer came in two separate pails later that day, I discovered the appetite I'd given up for death. The skin rubbed raw by my irons burned, but I was alive — and would stay so, at least for a time.

When the nightly visitations of rats came a-pattering, I thought of them for the first time, not as strangers, but as friends. Creatures, too, I supposed, could have death sentences commuted.

Before I shivered myself to sleep in my wad of straw, I told Mary Haydon and Catherine we'd live to see the morrow.

"And the one after that?" Catherine said.

"And after that?" said Mary Haydon.

"For what reason we don't know, we've been excused the death sentence."

Elizabeth Cole, whose cell was to the right of mine, said, "For stealing pottery-ware, I got seven years' transportation, like the rest of you. One month in the hulks and we'll all wish we had the hemp tight about our throats."

"The hulks?" said I.

"Them's prison ships," answered Elizabeth.

Only Elizabeth Cole seemed to know what the things called hulks really were. But she was of no mind to tell us more. She said, "You'll find out soon enough."

And so we did. Next morning, bright and early, and to the crying of the gulls, we were carried by cart to Devonport. There in the waterway lay the ship called *Dunkirk*.

"There she is," said Elizabeth Cole, her mouth drawn.

"It's a ship," I said hopefully.

"It ain't a movin' ship," Elizabeth Cole said.

"Then what kind is it?"

I drew my breath, as did Catherine and Mary Haydon.

"It's full of rats and holes and will sooner sink than sail."

After that, Elizabeth Cole spoke no more.

Presently, we were rowed out into the harbor. There we boarded the crusty, seaweed-sided, slimy old *Dunkirk*. With stumps for masts and decks littered with woeful shacks, the *Dunkirk* was more a wooden island than a seagoing vessel. And her smell was enough to make you quake. Belowdecks we heard men and women cackling, cursing, and crying.

Such was our introduction to the *Dunkirk,* which would be our permanent home, so far as we knew.

And thus it was that we exchanged a damp and dingy gaol cell for a damper and dingier one. Our quarters, tween decks, were dark as a dungeon; nine feet long, twenty inches wide for each prisoner.

Fortunately, for us women, the men were just going out to dredge the dockyards. This was their daily work, and highly prized it was.

I heard one man say, as he clanked up the stair, "A day out of the hulks is a day of birth."

Old men with white beards down to their bellies were among the line of convicts. Boys of tender years were close-clanked right in among them. Above the chiming chains there were the thin wails of lunatics begging to be flogged. In this terrible clamor we came into our narrow confines with trembling hands and dampened eyes.

I knew I'd never see my mother and father again. Nor my sister, nor any of the good green trees that were just now coming into leaf. I wept, as did the others, all of us hanging our heads and sobbing softly to the soughing of the waves against the hulk-ship.

I am loath to describe my surroundings. Had I the skill of a poet, I still wouldn't waste a word on such as this. Yet how else can I make you see the awfulness we lived in, day by day? No one bathed; everyone smelled. The odor of urine, sweat, and rottenness lay heavy in the air.

We'd now been afloat in this prison hulk for three months. The stink of the buckets of filth would kill an average person.

But we were average no more. We of the West Country were made tough, and though we grew thin and pale, we had our will.

I woke one night in the mild May air that came off the coast. For a moment I thought I was dreaming. I smelled the gorse, all a-bloom. I smelled the wet wool of rain-soft fleece, the aroma of a flock.

I smelled pilchards, salting in the sun, and the land smelled so dear to my heart. It took me back to my cousin Beth's wedding. . . .

Oh, how the wedding table groaned under the good spread of food. There was rabbit, stolen from one of the big estates, golden brown meat pies, cheeses, and smoked fish piled high. . . . Flagons of ale at the ready, and Beth, five or six months' forward with child, which is to say, not quite heavy with child, but with child, nonetheless. . . . How pretty with her posy of daisies, her muslin bonnet, arm in arm with her father . . . all of us heading for the white beribboned church gate . . . after the wedding and the long wayward noon of feasting, we let the food settle and then there was fiddling and dancing, kissing games and catching games, and a good deal of gossiping was had by all. . . . I don't think I was ever so happy in my life. . . .

Then to awaken with my hair full of nits and my body burning with lice. The odor of the hulk was as impenetrable as tar rising from the fog. How quickly it took away the sweet dream of my Fowey home.

By this time, my clothes were but rags. Fortunately for me, my leather gherkin didn't fall to pieces. But my man's trousers were split at the knee and torn in back. My ankles were rubbed raw from the irons, as was my waist from the iron belt that restrained me there.

I was a pretty picture, all ghostly pale and smutted with mold. Yet when I saw my close companions, Catherine and Mary Haydon, I scarce knew what to think. Their country dresses were fringed from the countless fights they'd had over stale bread. Sometimes our gaolers, the marines, would toss us extra rations. This, just to see the women fight over them.

More than half the women on the hulk were the mistresses of these gaolers. And, no matter how they looked coming in, they were rough wenches in a week's time, just like those women who leered under the lanterns and beckoned men with whispers and crooked fingers.

Well, on the hulk, there was no leering. Only suffering.

Came a morn when for what reason I don't remember, a marine named Watkin Tench helped me pour a necessary bucket over the deck railing. I suppose he saw I was too weak to do it by myself, and he risked his position to lend a hand.

That noon he brought me a meat broth, and seeing I was too weak to eat, he spoon-fed me like a baby. To the jeers of the starved and jealous, he took care of me. Thus the days went by, with him helping to nurse me back on my feet. None of the other officers seemed to notice or to care, so I suppose he bribed them off.

"Mary," he called one morning — he'd been caring for me a full week, by then. Out of the deep pocket of his red officer's coat he produced a huge iron key. Two clicks at the ankle and one at the waist, and I was light as goose down.

"Come on up top," said Mr. Tench, "and we'll see to your hair."

When the bright sun cracked my eyes, I shrank from it but he stood there shading me from the hurtful light.

Said he, "Don't worry, Mary, most of the other gaolers have gone ashore with the male convicts. Let me take you up and help you wash your hair."

Then he showed me something that caused the tears to flow like springwater. In an open box, he had a clean dress.

"It's too fine," I gasped. "I can't possibly wear it." His blue eyes shifted from me to the fine cotton dress, and then back to me. We were standing at the windward side near the rotten fo'c'sle. All about were the ramshackle shanties thrown up by the gaolers who slept on deck.

"Why not?" he questioned. His voice was softer than the cotton cloth he was giving me.

Well, it seemed most unbelievable. The blue sky overhead. The white sun on my shoulders. The salt air in my lungs.

But what price for all this? I wondered.

"Come, Mary," said Mr. Tench. "You can put the dress on later. Take this soap and water and get yourself good and clean."

He turned his back. But what cared I then? Whether he saw my flesh or not. I was a poor, beaten thing. As ugly as a wharf rat, but I was lucky and I knew it. I'd been chosen — and so I took up the soap and soon was clean.

The cold sea water burned the nit bites on my head. The lye soap stung my skin but shed the lice. My body was vibrating like a harp in the sunshine; and I think I cried, for no reason that I can remember. Mr. Tench couldn't tell the tears from the water. Hurriedly, my skin still wet, I put on the dress that meant greater freedom and . . . certain servitude. But as I said, it mattered not. For even now, as I heard the cries of the tween-decks prisoners below me, I felt myself to be different from them — some of them, anyway.

An exchange of sorts?

Yes, I believe it was such.

But glory be and God love Watkin Tench, for as I was soon to find out, a kinder man had never been born.

"Do you know where we're headed, Mary?"

I was combing out my dark brown hair with my fingers.

"They say we'll stay here until this barnacled heap rots into the bay," I told him.

Mr. Tench pointed his sharp chin at the horizon. He knelt beside me.

"You've really no clue, dear girl?"

I told him I didn't.

He reached into the same copious pocket that held the liberating key and produced a russet apple.

"Here," he offered, balancing the apple on his fist.

I snatched it from him, bit into it, and the sweet goodness filled my mouth.

"That's my little shack over there," he mentioned.

I had some qualms about going inside, but I took the hand he offered. He felt as warm as I was cold. Then he saw me shivering there in front of his hut made of diverse wood scraps patched together like a tawdry quilt.

"Not much to look at," he said, dropping my hand.

I peeked in; it had no door and was merely a lean-to of sorts. Yet to me, who'd lived in that tween-decks hell, it seemed a castle on the cliffs of Dover.

One night, late, the sky graying toward morn, I chanced
to overhear my Mr. Tench conversing with another marine.
They were smoking pipes at the time, slightly aft of his hut.
Supposedly I was asleep as he'd left me. But something in
the way he rose roused me to wake. The slap and gentle
thud of the tide was heard betwixt their voices, which stayed
at a level, shiplap lull, just above a whisper.

"Have we been assigned yet?" asked an unfamiliar voice.
Peeking through the doorway of our hut, I saw the lantern-
bright faces of Mr. Tench and his nameless friend. They held
a match to the lit bowls of their pipes.

"All I hear," Mr. Tench said, "is some tale about the glo-
ries of Botany Bay."

"That's the truth," spoke the other, a cloud of fragrant
smoke rising over his head and mingling with the points of
stars.

"When will we heave up anchors then?" Mr. Tench asked.

The mariner shifted his position, resting his elbows on
the portside railing, so I could barely hear him.

"Most likely when all the transports are fitted up." He
paused and went on. "There'll be some ten ships, I'm told.
They'll vary in tonnage, but roughly from two hundred
seventy-five to three hundred fifty tons, every one of them
packed to the gunnels with convicts."

"How many convicts all together?"

"One thousand and twenty."

The mariner puffed on his pipe. Then, turning around and taking the pipe from his mouth, he pointed the stem at Mr. Tench. "You've seen the maps of New Holland, I take it."

"No," Mr. Tench avowed, "but I once had a look at Cook's log. New Holland's a very long way off. Six months or more out in the Dutch East Indies."

The mariner tapped his pipe bowl against the rail. "The Home Secretary," he said, "has ordered the convicts out of here — to be rid of them — forever."

For . . . ever . . .

The word, or words, stuck in my mind.

Could it really be? Would I be banished, then, for stealing a bonnet? Well, better, I should say, than to be hung by the neck until dead.

In the weeks that followed, I picked up even more talk about the disposal of us convicts. It was true. We were to be shipped off, just as the mariner said. I tried to imagine this nearly spent Devonshire girl, myself, traveling to such a narrow corner of the globe.

Botany Bay, they called it. Yet, despite the awfulness of the long and torturous voyage, I imagined the place was pretty.

All hope of that prettiness faded, though, when I considered the sinkable hulk we were chained to. What if she should sink right there in the harbor? We'd go down like a bag of stones. Each week, as batches of new prisoners arrived, I saw how dreadfully loaded down we were. Barely out of water.

One night when Mr. Tench had no time for me, I lay enchained beside Catherine and Mary Haydon. There was one position only for a side sleeper. The iron belt around my waist had to rest in a knothole I had gouged out so as to keep me from rocking.

It was too dark to see Catherine's face, but I heard her voice quite clear. "Mary, do you know yet what's to become of us?"

"Too dire for words," I answered. "We're to be transported to New Holland."

"What's that got to do with Botany Bay?"

"It's the same stupefying place," I answered.

From over Catherine's shoulder, I heard Mary Haydon. "One wretchedness is the same as another," she observed. "And whether they break our spirit here, or there, is of no consequence to me."

"Don't either of you understand?" I argued. "It's the place Captain Cook went. Where the fruit hangs ripe on the trees."

"Nonsense," said Mary Haydon. "It's a barren, nasty island inhabited by dangerous savages."

"Cannibals," Catherine put in.

"Well, I don't know about you two," said I, "but I'd rather rot in the open air of an island than stay tween decks and fade away like this."

Catherine turned, her chains noisily clinking.

"A lifer's likely to get commuted," she said, sighing. "But in forsaken Botany Bay, what's the hope of getting a good-conduct pardon? Face it, we're prisoners for life."

"Life," Mary Haydon said, and started to cry.

"Will you shut your mouths?" someone yelled. It was one of the older women.

"Yeah," cried another.

The irons began to clink.

On the other side of our barricaded cellblock, the male prisoners had their ears tuned on our words, and with their eyes they preyed on our every movement.

So we settled down, thinking our own private thoughts.

I knew more than I could tell. My privilege above decks afforded me the luxury of knowing things. I knew, for instance, there was a sloop named the *Nautilus* that had already explored the coast of Africa, looking for a place to dump us. But that distant coast proved desolate and unfit. King George thought it better to go to Botany Bay, which was said to be a nicer place.

I'd gleaned plenty of rumors from Mr. Tench and his friends. Rumors of wars, disposals of convicts, rumors of colonies, and what not. What I'd learned of Botany Bay was mostly to the good. The marines didn't seem to despise their assignment. So why should we? As I saw it, anything was preferable to the deathlike conditions of the *Dunkirk*.

The Hulk

January 1787

I counted the days and scored them with my thumbnail in the sideboard, where I rested my head at night. We'd spent nine horrible months on the *Dunkirk*. Much of my pain was lessened by Mr. Tench's kindness. I worked the less and rested the more. But now that we were off that hulk and on the *Charlotte,* Mr. Tench was closely watched, so he was unable to spare me any pains. I was back tween decks and in the dark all the time.

The weather had us in a bad way. They said we'd have been on our way if it weren't for some delay with supplies. The things we needed hadn't arrived yet — so there we were, waiting again.

One night, after we had been on the *Charlotte* for a few weeks, Mr. Tench came below and visited me. "I'm being watched," he said. But then he unlocked my chains. I rubbed my sores. The red flesh was very tender.

"Can we — ?"

"No going above for a breath of wind," he warned.

Shortly after, he said he had to hitch me in again, and I started to cry, but held it back.

In the brief brilliance of Mr. Tench's lantern, I saw a face staring at me through the iron grate that divided the men from

the women. A face so lonely and full of longing that you'd remember it a lifetime, if you saw it. Dark and handsome.

After being locked up, I lay down and tried to sleep. Mr.
Tench went up the ladder, taking his golden light with him.

Below him the shadows raced after one another. Tween
decks turned dark as a tomb. I lay still trying to focus my
memory on that face. I was stuck on the dark hollows of
those eyes. I couldn't shake the thought of him. I'd known
him somewhere.

But who was he?

I lay there with the irons biting into my sores. The nits attacked my head, but I paid them no mind. You learn to live
with pains and aches, sickness and hunger — or you don't
live at all. I pushed these natural enemies of mine away, and
concentrated on the face.

Who in thunder was he?

It came to me of a sudden: He was of Irish folk.

How did I know *that*?

I saw his milky skin, his sunken cheeks, his grayish eyes,
and darkish locks. Oh, but I knew him! Yet from *where*?

If I'd been in my bed at home, I'd have tossed and
turned, trying to recollect. However, here, I had no choice
but to be flat, or lie to the side. Flat it was, that night.

Someone, two pallets down, cried out in her sleep, "Oh,
Johnny."

A kind of cackle followed. Some snores. Silence. The slapping of the tide, shuffle of feet above decks. More silence.

That face wouldn't let go of me, or I wouldn't let go of it.

Either way, I wasn't getting any sleep because of it.

And then it came to me in a rush.

Will Bryant!

The same as lived with his family on the Isle of Wight. Smugglers, they were, too. The whole family. It was some years ago I'd met him — if, in fact, a meeting it was.

My father had been called out one night to help unload a lugger in the cove. They worked by moonlight, so as to not arouse suspicion.

There were several men there, as well as my father. All were apprehensive, as I recall, for the men of the Preventive Service were always about Fowey, looking for thieves. And these they were, hardened by years of salvage. Taking from the claws of the sea whatever she'd render up: barrels of liquor, arms, silk from the Orient. And often, stores of food useful for such as us: hardtack and the like.

This night they moved like clockwork in the secrecy of the cove, well cloaked. Their moon-pale faces were remembered by me, though. In the gruff whispers of the crew, there was a singular voice of one who was not yet a man.

I, being but fifteen or so, harkened to the sound. Then to the face that I could see whenever he stepped out from under the bundle he was toting. How I liked the look of him. He was not betrayed, as yet, by hard knocks, and he had the look of the altar boy about him. His dark hair framed the comely face nicely. I thought it strange, him looking like a cherub but carrying a man's cutlass at his side.

I was there to keep watch. To see that no one came along the road from Fowey to Solcombe. And this I did right well — when I wasn't staring into the moonlit face of Will Bryant.

My father gave me his name ere we cracked our door. I saw naught of him again, just that once. But he'd stayed with me. And, there he was, the same lad. All grown up and manly, and hanging his chin on an iron prison bar.

And looking at me.

I wondered, did *he* remember that night long ago?

He couldn't have seen but a glimpse of me, if that. I wore a man's sailing hat, a cap with the brim down over my eyes. Nor could he have known I had a girl's head of hair, for it was tied up, hidden.

Will Bryant.

How could he know that I offered him my heart that night?

The Charlotte

April 1787

We moldered four months tween decks on the *Charlotte*.

Spring came and one night I dreamed of daffodils. Perhaps I smelled real ones offshore, I don't know.

Well, the hills around Fowey were aglow with flowers then, though I couldn't see them. Our little forest hiding place was in full leaf. I thought of the small packet of pressed flowers and autumn leaves that I'd left in our little earthen lean-to. Most likely, they were turned to rot from the rains. But I liked to think they were still there, as I'd left them. How lovely to think of some wayward boy finding that secret spot: our charcoals, our tin of water, our pallets grown over with moss.

I tied some ribbons to a low branch. It would have been nice to have them now for my hair.

Mr. Tench's attentions, so to put it, hadn't been very regular. He was being watched, I know. But still, I'd gotten used to that weekly bath. The nits were eating me alive. And poor Catherine, always groaning in her sleep. She slept through the pain, as most were wont to do.

Mary Haydon looked so gray from lack of light.

So must I have seemed myself.

You cannot know what it meant to be removed from the grace of the sun. To never see the light except when the hatchway was cracked — and then the suddenness of the sun was too stunning, and it hurt beyond measure.

We heard rumors about a mass sickness on the *Lady Penrhyn,* the ship moored aft of us. Sailors and prisoners from the *Charlotte* were put aboard her to scrub and fumigate the decks, while we did the same.

"I hear they're up to their elbows in quicklime," Catherine told me. For us, another day of scrubbing in the dark. Working in the sour reek of vomit. On all fours, chains scraping, brushes chuffing.

The round of deaths tween decks was constant. As we cleaned, we often turned up a new corpse. The *Charlotte* — as well as the *Penrhyn* — was a death ship.

"What does Mr. Tench tell you?" Mary Haydon asked as we worked.

"He thinks we'll sail away soon."

"Soon, soon," sang Catherine. "That's all I ever hear."

We were, all three of us, elbow to elbow. No light, not even a candle. And the unpardonable stench of death in the air — if air you'd call it.

My stomach was very uneasy that morning, I recall.

"Mr. Tench hardly speaks to me anymore," I said. "All I know's, the poor man's not been paid for his work. There's word that a mutiny's going to spark unless the marines are given their back pay."

"I call that the usual scuttle," said Catherine. "They're killing us, but the poor dears aren't being paid for their murdering ways. How unfair."

Said a raspy voice, "Murderers don't get paid unless they're in the infantry."

"Who's that speaking?" I asked.

"No one you'd know," came the cackling reply. "And better that way, darling. For we're all bound for the same place, and I don't mean Botany Bay, like they say."

"What is your meaning, then?" came Mary Haydon.

"Figure it, yourself, honey. They use and abuse us, as they like. Then when we're sick to death, they cast us off like the vermin we are."

"Ahh!" came another voice, trailing in the shadows.

"What you was saying before," Catherine whispered, pressing close to me, so I could feel the weight of her chains beside my knees.

"About what?"

"About the scrubbing going on over to the *Lady Penrhyn*."

"What of it?"

"If you heard what I heard, you'd know, that if we ever

get out of this harbor, it'll be a bloody miracle. They're dying like flies over there. Today, the marines are throwing quick-lime on the decks, and bodies out into the harbor."

"Do they burn them first?"

"Sometimes, they burn a little juniper to kill the stink. But the bodies just feed the sharks."

"How do you know this?"

She said nothing. My heart was jumping. All of a sudden, I felt terribly sick. We'd finished scrubbing and the floor must've been clean — at least in our quarter — because the cockroaches had stopped biting us.

The ship was rocking. Swaying. I dug my fingernails into the deck. My head reeled. The unpleasantness spread in a sickening wave all down my body, causing a kind of humming noise in my ears. Then, I just flopped over, and was dead to the world.

When I woke, my head was on Catherine's knee.

"What's happened to me?" I asked.

"You were sick, Mary."

"I still don't feel good."

"Is it the fever?" Catherine asked.

Then it all came startlingly clear. It wasn't a disease.

I was going to have a baby.

I made my resolve in that dark hold and with the ship

creaking under us: They'd not kill me, nor my child. They'd not put me in the sea for shark bait. I'd survive. I'd live, and the baby in me would grow strong. These convictions raced across my mind as the sickness in my stomach passed.

That night, Mr. Tench unchained me. He brought me up on deck to breathe the fresh sea air.

I drank that air as deep as I could get it, down to my toes.

"You know I've been watched," said Mr. Tench.

I looked at him for the first time in months, surprised at his ruddy good looks in the lantern light. Brownish hair, fine teeth, and eyes evenly spaced.

I didn't love him. I trusted him.

He said, after some silence, "The Head of Expedition is Captain Phillip."

"Is he the one who's been watching you?"

"No, that's Captain Gilbert."

"How can I tell them apart? I don't ever get up here to see anyone anymore."

"You've been in that hellish hold so long, and there was nothing I could do. I wish I could've done something — anything would've been better than nothing. But this Captain Gilbert doesn't approve of our being friendly like this. He wants no breach of etiquette, no niceness of any kind."

"Does that mean we cannot even speak?"

He turned to the stern of the *Charlotte* and glanced at the nightwatch, who was standing at attention, his firing piece resting on his shoulder. At the bows there was another guard, this one pacing to and fro.

"Even now there's eyes on us."

"I can live with that."

He nodded, smiled. "Of course."

"No matter what, I have to stay alive."

He saw the urgency in my eyes.

"You don't have to worry on that account, Mary . . . as long as I am here."

"But now you must watch over the two of us, for I am going to have a baby . . . no, *we* are going to have a baby, Mr. Tench."

Hearing this, he changed not one whit. His face like rock. As if he hadn't heard what I had said.

"Do you hear me?"

Far off in the night, a heron croaked. An iron, bleaky sound. Way away in the shoals, a light blinked. Suddenly, I remembered Will Bryant. His keen, gray eyes.

Mr. Tench interrupted my thoughts. "I heard you, Mary. I always hear what you say."

His voice was apologetic.

"I'm bound to my work. Were it not that way, I'd've shipped off, like a lot of others. Did you know that many of the mariners quit duty, went landward with their complaints?

So, then, every hothead was let go. I was one of the quiet ones. But look now. I've been paid and I've a new uniform, Mary. Did you notice?"

Of course, I'd seen the new clothing he had on. The bright blue coat and white trousers. Yet, for all my good wishes to him who was my savior I saw myself, too — there I was, still in chains. Filthy. The dress he'd given me black as coal. A pitiful mess, I was . . . and him in a spanking new uniform.

Was I lovely once? Yes, I think I was. But I don't really remember.

"So you're with child," said Mr. Tench.

He made it sound common — well, maybe it was. As I was, too.

But how could he be so indifferent?

A coldness crept into me.

Mr. Tench made as if to touch me, but then withdrew his hand.

"I'm up to here with pity, Mary," he said, touching his throat. "There's nothing I can do for you — yet. Let us bide our time and see what's to be done."

"We have only six months to bide, as you say. I'm going to need extra rations."

"I'd give you my own, if they'd let me."

I wondered if he really meant it.

"This Captain Gilbert is a cruel one."

"No." He shook his head, came closer. I felt him touch my cheek with his hand.

The two guards were just then out of sight.

"Don't worry, I'll see to it you don't starve."

"And our baby?"

"I'll do what I can, as always. The truth is, Captain Phillip wants to keep the prisoners alive. He doesn't want them dropped into the harbor in shrouds."

"Pray, why not? The way we're being treated, I'd've thought that's *all* he wanted."

I looked into the harbor and I saw what seemed to be a four-master, etched against the moonlit clouds.

"You people are going to colonize New Holland, Mary."

"What good's that? I mean, the likes of *us* —"

He came closer; I smelled the trace of warm rum on his breath.

"You're all to the good. Once we get there, you'll see. You people will be the future of Botany Bay Colony. All of England wants to see this happen, wants to see it work. And if it *does* work, it'll be a grand experiment, don't you think?"

I searched his eyes and said, "How pretty to think you can experiment with human lives."

He sighed. "I don't think you quite understand."

"Nor do you, Mr. Tench. But let's not ruin the fresh

breeze with trifles. I'll live and you'll help me. That way the baby inside me will grow up and not know the nightmare that I'm living in. It's for that I'm going to stay alive, and be your very best Mary."

He grinned, rubbed his cheek, and said, "Brave girl."

Then, saying no more, he took me below and chained me to my quarter.

The next morning, we were called upon to rise above, and hear the Head of Expedition, Captain Phillip, give us a great welcome speech. He spoke briskly in his cherry red uniform and slick white pants. Grand and important, he walked the length of the *Charlotte*, addressing all of us. I must say, even I thought him somewhat splendid. It was the air he had, powerful and swift. His sharp chin nobly cocked, his hands behind his back as he spoke, clearly and with a rich, baritone voice.

"I know the conditions have been appalling, and many of you are sick. As soon as we set sail you will be allowed daily walks on the deck, and if the weather is good, there is no reason you should not spend even more time in the fresh air. I must warn you, this will depend on your good behavior. Nothing out of the ordinary will be tolerated. Do you understand?"

Captain Phillip stopped speaking. My eyes fell to his magnificent footwear. High booted, his leather gave off a shine like polished ebony. He was staring at us, seeming to see us. The marines had always looked right through us, as if we weren't there. But this man, this glorious captain, was meeting our gaze.

Suddenly, I felt a glowing all around my heart. I vowed, then, to never risk the privilege thus proffered. I stared at this exalted, golden, embroidered man. He was just a man, of course. But, to me, and possibly to others, he was something more, something greater, perhaps.

He resumed his speech.

"You people are our bid, that is, England's hope for the Great Empire abroad."

His eyes traveled around the deck trying to capture and hold each and every face.

"I think he really means it," whispered Catherine. There was some light in her eyes for the first time in all these many months; looking around I saw in more than a few faces the same look of hope. There was charity in his words and, I hoped, in his heart. Could he really mean it? Could it really be true? Maybe then we weren't just convicts — pitiful demons who had stolen a crust of bread in order to live.

Maybe we were human beings after all.

Voyage

A strong westerly wind had delayed our departure, but finally in May we were leaving — the *Sirius,* the *Lady Penrhyn,* the *Friendship,* the *Scarborough,* and the *Charlotte,* all of us together as a fleet of ships.

From the wards of Portsmouth there were but few to see us off. I saw neither my mother nor my sister through the slit at portside.

I witnessed no sorrowful farewells — some of us, the women in particular, grew cheery as the seamen heaved up the anchors and set sail.

Still, when I saw the cliffs of Wight disappear, a sudden tear streaked down my cheek. However, as the canvas creaked overhead whilst the bare feet of the seamen clapped above decks, and everyone cheered, I said to Mary Haydon, "This is no better than a slaver's hold in the middle passage."

Said Catherine, "Do you ever wonder why they have us in irons? I mean, are we women desperate and so dangerous?"

"Well," I said, "when we clear the Channel, they're going to remove the irons of the men so they can work above decks."

Catherine continued, "They've got us in chains for other

reasons, as you all well know. So they can take us when it pleases them."

On that score, I said nothing of the trade I'd made. I had less weevily bread than the other women ate, which, by the way, I shared because I always looked to the welfare of others, and not just myself. In turn, they shared their little riches with me — sometimes fruit and a little sugarcane.

Our conditions worsened. In the night, below decks was harsh and suffocating. Often I closed my eyes tight and pictured the sea curling on the cobble at Solcombe. Or I imagined the heather come into flower, and the lambs of snowy wool. That way, despite the blood-drawing nits in my hair, I somehow managed to sleep. And dreamed of fair-eyed Will Bryant.

Some weeks passed by. Captain Marshall of the *Friendship* reported that there was a plot among his prisoners to overthrow his ship, and ours. Mr. Tench and many of the marines went to capture the ringleaders of this uprising.

All of us women peered anxiously through the slits, wondering what would happen.

Then some shots cracked. We knew at once that men would be hung at the yardarm that same day. Instead, two forlorn and shadowy figures were hauled to the *Charlotte* and given six dozen lashes each. We were brought above decks to witness the punishment.

First the men were chained to a grating and then flogged by two of our drummers, boys scarcely old enough to deliver these cruel blows — but they did. The spectacle was dreadful, and one I can't forget.

Captain Phillip said, "There shall be no further signs of mutiny from this day of sailing until the time we cast anchor in Botany Bay. Your demeanor will be on the whole humble and regular. Is this understood by each and every soul present?"

We nodded, mutely and glumly. I noticed droplets of blood falling through the grate and spattering on the dirty straw where we slept.

The following day, one of our youngest, a girl who had lived close to my home, became mysteriously ill, fell feverish, and by the midnight bell was dead. When this knowledge was given to a guard, he quickly told the news to Captain Phillip, who ordered the girl to be buried at sea forthwith. As she had on a scanty frock that was all torn to fringe, I begged Mr. Tench to find a bit of ragged sailcloth for her shroud. He said there was none, and that I should know better than to ask.

So, here was a pretty girl I'd once seen milking cows near my home thrown into the sea, and that was the end of her. But once she was the princess of her parents' eyes.

June 1787

Mr. Tench was the one who told me that we'd arrived at Tenerife in the Canary Islands. He needn't have said a word, though. For as we lay in the night port, the land wind ferried the smells of seaweed rotting on the beach. Toward dawn came more odors — sun on sand, and the sweetness of herbage.

Above decks, I saw a different Mr. Tench. He seemed to have resumed his old confident air. Indeed, he saw my soiled dress, the one he had given me some months before, as if for the first time. Blinking in surprise, he said, "Why, Mary, that thing's no better than a filthy rag."

"And what do you expect? I am in filth all day long."

"With good behavior that will change."

"How can we exercise bad behavior, I want to know? We're women . . . and in chains."

He scratched his head, and his eyes blinked in the white light of Tenerife. I looked about at the sky and the sea — one was the bluest of blues, and the other bested it.

Said Mr. Tench, "We're to get a grog allowance, we marines. You'll get a pound of beef each, plus a light quantity of soft bread."

"Is it really so?"

He nodded in earnest. "It is, Mary. This is a fine, rich port."

A little later he was called off to duty, but when he returned, he thrust some cloth into my hands. On top of it he put a big, round, golden, gorgeous orange. I shivered with surprise when I sniffed the fruit. It smelled clean and sweet and wholesome.

The other gift, as it turned out, was a broadcloth shirt of Mr. Tench's, long enough in length to hang past my knees, and so clean as to still have the starch in it.

Days passed in port. The stores of food kept coming; we were allowed to see them without chains. Already the salt air was having a healthy effect on the iron sores on my ankles and waist. The shirt-dress billowed in the wind off Santa Cruz Harbor and flapped against my legs.

We were quickly cumbered up with stores, so much so that there was hardly anywhere to stand. The gun deck was so cluttered with crates of chickens that we were unable to salute the marquis of Branceforte, the governor of Tenerife, when he came to visit us.

I'd never seen foreigners such as these. I'm bound to say that the black-whiskered nobles who came aboard were splendid-handsome. Not so great to my mind as Will Bryant, but good-looking enough in their own way to stand out in the sun and make us pay attention to their every little movement.

Day after day was spent in putting up provisions, and we

women prisoners helped right alongside the men, and did as good a job, too.

I got tired rather sooner than some of the others. Not something I was used to experiencing — for my belly was turning out and beginning to bulge — but I worked around it.

Yet the most notable event of Tenerife was the shot fired by a sentry at the gangway. This was accompanied by the news that a prisoner named Joseph Powell had gotten away from the *Scarborough*. Immediately, boats were lowered, and a frantic search of the harbor was started.

Mary Haydon, whilst leaning at the rail next to me, said, "I hear the captain of the *Scarborough*'s under penalty of forty pounds for every man who escapes him."

"From the way he's yelling at his rowers, I've no doubt it's true," said I.

Then there was a call for the rowers to stop. All oars were raised and dripping. Some marksmen in the boats aimed their long guns along the shoreline. We drew a breath and said a small prayer.

My eyes saw him first.

"There he is by the foot of that great rock."

"Is it Powell?"

"Him, if anyone."

He was trying to climb the rock. But each time he got up on it, the pounding surf grabbed him and pulled him back

down. So, at last, he crumpled, too tired to move, and let the
water wash over him.

Catherine asked, "Is he dead?"

"Only weary — still holding on," I answered.

The marksmen prepared to fire. But we heard the captain
of the *Scarborough* shout out, "Not until I give the order, men."

The marines lowered their long guns. They seemed to go
slack in the shoulders whilst the captain called out to the fugitive.

"Powell! You surrender?"

What could he do else? The poor, washed-up thing didn't
utter a word. The foam splashed over him. His face was
streaked with blood. He stared toward us with all those guns
upon him. The marines were a trigger's pull away from send-
ing his soul aloft.

Then a dinghy rode in beside the rock where Powell
stood, shoulder deep in the salt water. For a moment I thought
he was going to dive under and try to get away. Yet he stayed
fixed, wobbly but unmoving.

Said the captain to his men, "He's finished running. Get
him." Powell's face — how shall I ever forget it? He was
already a dead man, and knew it.

Finally, he was brought aboard the *Charlotte*. The next
day he was punished for the private enjoyment of Captain
Phillip, and then we were summoned to see him beaten once
again. He was given twelve dozen and sent, with his back all

shredded, to his own ship, where, we heard, he was lashed a third time for the benefit of his fellow prisoners.

We later heard that his irons were doubled and tripled until he couldn't move an inch, and in that condition, he bled to death.

I vowed, on my unborn child, that I would deliver her or him into a world that was better than this. A world of love, not retribution.

Less than a week later, there was another tragic incident. One of the convicts was a coiner, and he was given a secret license to practice his villainy. This all came about because the mariners took kindly to the fruit of Santa Cruz — that is, not the kind that grows on trees, but the kind that is shaped like a woman.

These island delicacies and the local rum delivered the men to the action I'm telling of, and a terrible thing grew out of their foolishness.

You see, these selfsame mariners hadn't the wherewithal to buy anything. They were all owed months of back-pay. So they were as poor as could be.

Catherine said one day that her marine was responsible for setting up this coiner with a bunch of pewter spoons. From these the clever fellow made Santa Cruzan silver dollars. The coiner was paid for his cleverness with an ample stock of tobacco, and the deal was done.

However, the first attempt to pass the coins failed. The marines, to save themselves from Captain Phillip, confessed the whole plot . . . but blamed it on the coiner.

The worst that happened to the sailors was their grog was stopped. But the coiner suffered a double punishment: He was flogged until his flesh was rent. Then he was cursed and spat upon by sailors and prisoners alike for losing those precious spoons. He was despised and made into a scapegoat.

After some more days in port, the *Charlotte* set sail for Rio de Janeiro of the Brazils.

The sky turned foul on the way. We felt it churning neath the keel. We rolled and shipped water; and bailed and shipped more. At night, under the hull, we heard the strange songs of sirens — Catherine said, "Beasts of the deep."

I cared not what it was as we pitched and rolled so long as we stayed afloat, which I dearly prayed for. That night I comforted myself with the notion that I'd spoken to Will Bryant.

And — he'd almost spoken back to me.

"Do you remember who I am?" I asked.

He gave me a little thin-lipped smile.

So after leaving the Canary Islands — and having never seen a single canary whilst there — I was swabbing the deck along with some of the other women. We were all on hands and knees when I overheard some news that passed between Mr. Tench and another marine, Lieutenant Fairfax.

"Say, Tench, whatever became of that girl with the sad brown eyes?"

Catherine glanced at me, raised her eyebrows.

I listened.

"She's still on the list, among the living."

"I could've sworn you were sweet on her," the lieutenant said.

"Well, I may have been a little sentimental toward her," Mr. Tench replied indifferently.

The lieutenant rambled on. "I heard they chained and dumped Powell in the sea."

"The worse for him and that coiner, too."

"By the by, Tench, would the girl have *none* of you — or *all* of you?"

Mr. Tench coughed. "What's it to you, Fairfax?"

"I just want to know if you're a *man*."

"I am, and good day, sir."

Was I to think that he was a gentleman? That he loved me? Nay, some heartsick child could've thought so, but I knew the man I dealt with, and he was neither brave nor great, but as he himself said, a man.

Mr. Tench was like any of us — a little better, maybe.

He wouldn't dirty his career for me, that I knew. His mil-

itary standing meant everything to him. Below that, I was
somewhere in his thoughts. But what I really meant to him, I
will never know for certain.

The end of June was almost on us — and so was the tropic heat.

So far, our sailing weather was desperate rough. We
pitched and rolled, day and night. The women — hardy though
we were — were sick much of the time.

We had extra rations, but what use? They wound up on
the pitching floor . . . a meal relished by the *millers* . . . those
stinking rats that crawl amongst our straws and feed on our
excrement.

I'd given up hearing tattler's tales . . . they bore nothing
but the brunt of bad news. However, lately, whilst waxing
the wheel, I chanced to hear how the ship's in such rotten
condition that we're apt to sink in the swells. "The rascally
navy yard contractors," the marine said, "it's a wonder she
don't roll her decks out, guns and all."

Shortly after I digested this flip-flap, Catherine came to
me with other terrible tidings.

We were chained in for the night, and she got close —
Mary Haydon being on t'other side for once (she snores) —
and whispered in the dampish dark after the guard had gone
above decks with his pipe, "I hear some boxes of candles
were broached by a few of our men . . . so a marine secreted

himself near the forward bulkhead near the crew's quarters, and he overheard a plot about how some of the convicts were going to seize the ship."

"Is — Will Bryant — any part of it?" I asked.

Catherine near choked at this. "You've already got one man . . . isn't that enough for you, Mary Broad?"

"Keep it down," I reminded her. "Someone'll be listening."

She got her head very near mine, so that our foreheads were bumping with the ship's rocking to and fro, and then she said, hoarse and soft, her breath smelling of rotten canker, "Our boys had not only gotten their hands on candles but on crowbars, too. But, as I was saying, that no-good guard got a hold of this news and the men were searched and found out, and that's why we saw those four fellows leave yesterday morning."

"Where did they take them?"

"They keelhauled them; ran them the length of the *Sirius* so their backs were torn up by the barnacles. Then, half-drowned, they were drug up on deck and ringbolted to dry. They're there still, if you want to know."

"No one gets away, but one day I will."

"I hope I don't live to see you get caught," she answered dryly.

After that I contented myself with the hope that Will lived to see the day so that the two of us could escape together.

August 1787

We came at last to Rio de Janeiro. Yet though we were in sight of the mountains, we weren't allowed to go above decks. We smelled the flowers growing by the sea, yet we couldn't see them. We heard the donkeys bray and the roosters crow, yet our eyes were unmet by them. These were out of range of our peephole, and we lived — night and day — in the tween-decks twilight. In our ears the weedy sea wash slapped the hull of the *Charlotte,* and was our song of constant sorrow.

Mr. Tench and his fellow marines were mad to go ashore, and so our best hope, in the foulness of our irons, was that they'd bring us back some fresh fruit. Our teeth ached for the lack of it.

I was so heavy now that walking was well nigh impossible. Yet the weight of the chains made my despair all the more painful and uneasy, so that I rested not, but tossed and turned from side to side. I worried all the time: What should follow if I died giving birth? Who would raise my child?

The days went by with the same boredom as before — whether in harbor or at sea, we were in the dark. Each day more supplies were brought back to the ship; fresh vegetables, fruit, and salted meat. Every night the marines went ashore and had their fun — sometimes we heard them laughing drunkenly. One night there were voices of women and strains of music from a guitar. How I longed to be a part of that music, that freedom.

After some more days and nights of lying about in the blistering heat, the *Charlotte* — fully loaded with stores — left this port and journeyed on to the Cape of Good Hope.

I now began to take stock of my chances for survival.

More and more convicts were sick.

We had food — but, alas, many were unable to eat it. My chances of having an easy childbirth, I believed, were slim. As nothing was easily given hereabouts and most everyone was sick to the stomach and feverish with the ague, I wondered what my hopes were pinned upon — the ship's surgeon, Dr. John White, wanted to see my baby live. And by some miracle, I remained well — but for how long?

None of the women I was with had knowledge of babies, or bearing them; worse, most were gray-faced with illness. I'd been a midwife with my mother, who was often called upon in Fowey to assist with births, but that seemed so long ago. What I remembered, mostly, was the pained faces of those mothers whose babes were born in death's embrace — and buried before they breathed their first draft of air.

Dr. White finally came to see me.

"Will you remove these chains for my birth?"

"We shall see," was all he said. His eyes evaded me.

What if he said no? Those hateful ankle chains were scarce eighteen inches apart. They cut into my skin. When I moved they caused much pain.

In the dead of night when we heard the crying of the wind, my child pushed hard, and kicked.

How could I blame him, or her, for wanting out — that was what I wanted, too. But I was caught between iron and flesh, wood and sea, heaven and earth. And so was my pretty little unborn baby.

October 1787

🚢 I was the news all about the ship — the entire convoy, for that matter. Rowdy good cheers were sent up with flags right after the announcement that a baby girl — the firstborn to the First Fleet — was on board the *Charlotte*. Of this I must confess: I was too tired to take much heart in the celebration.

I was warned by Mr. Tench that it would be best, all things considered, to marry quickly, and thus secure a future on Botany Bay. Married women, Captain Phillip said, would receive the best treatment — rations, shelter, and so on.

Yet who am I to marry? Mr. Tench, when I asked him, said, "I haven't any intention of that." We were above decks, that day, looking out on a spacious, calm sea.

"Mightn't you do it, for the sake of the child?" I asked.

There was, I knew, a pathetic and pleading sound to my voice that I had tried unsuccessfully to hide.

He put his hand on my shoulder. "As unwelcome though it may be to your ears, Mary, I am due to wed back in Portsmouth when I return."

The wind ruffled his hair, and his gray eyes seemed steel to me then, with nothing back of them but dour and selfish thoughts. In another instant, my father's French-Irish temper, which lived so deep in my heart, went by, and I forgave him, fully. After all, he was doing the best he could, and so was I.

"You know, Mary," Mr. Tench said, taking up his heavy hand and putting it into the pocket of his officer's coat, "you might try *elsewhere* . . ."

I glanced up quickly at him.

"You mean — marry someone else?"

"For the child's own good, as well as yours."

He had, perhaps, read my mind. The one I really wanted was behind bars and in chains. He was, truly, my heart's fancy.

"May I have the right to wed a — convict — on this ship, then?"

"Captain Phillip has given his word that it may happen," said Tench. He took out his pipe and lighted it with his back to the wind. "If you have someone in mind, Mary, I'll take your request directly to him."

I started to say who my truelove was, but I stammered when it came to mouthing the name of Will Bryant. For what if he wouldn't have me? I'd seen him watching me from afar, even staring insolently through the grating that separated us. Yet, at other times, he was naught but goodness, looking so much the same lad of that night in the smuggler's cave long ago.

Did he really know me?

What if this was just a wild ride of my fancy?

I confess, ever since giving birth to Charlotte, the strangest things came into my head . . . deliriums, Catherine called them.

We came then to the Cape of Good Hope, and to Cape Town. Once again we were stocking up on fresh provisions: meat, fruit, vegetables, bread, and this time, plenty of livestock — so many animals, in fact, that the above decks was crowded with donkeys, cattle, sheep, chickens, pigs, ducks, and, it seemed Noah's Ark, with no room for any of us prisoners.

These burdens lumbered our ship up very much, as well as all the others in the fleet.

The day we anchored, Myneer Von de Graffe, the Dutch governor at the Cape, came on board. He was a fine, soldiery looking man with amber whiskers and genial eyes. The first man we've seen of white skin who wasn't fearful of looking into our faces.

He took a special interest in me, as I had a babe in arms — now a christened babe, at that.

"What is the child's name, dear?" Mr. Von de Graffe queried under his huge, straw-colored eyebrows.

"Her name is Charlotte," I told him.

"Appropriate. And how is it that you were transported? You don't look to be a criminal."

It pained me to speak of this in front of such a fine and

honest gentleman, but I did speak up accordingly. "I was sentenced for stealing a bonnet," I said.

Captain Phillip, who was standing nearby, grimaced. He liked it not — this palavering.

"For a bonnet, did you say?" He seemed astonished.

Mutely, I nodded.

"As long as you're in these protected waters, dear lady, I decree that you shall wear no chain upon your leg. Further, you shall go free about the ship as if you were" — he paused, glanced about the animal-crowded deck, and finished — "not one of these brutes."

"Very well, sir," Captain Phillip seconded from the fo'c'sle. He looked much chagrined, and he turned to other things straightaway.

All that day I went about at my ease. A little guiltily perhaps. But I got over that. Once, I was offered a drink of tea by a marine I didn't know. However, the other women turned away from me, and I heard their chains chinking, reminding me of who I was. That night when I was chained in myself, I was relieved to be thus encumbered.

Strange to say, I was one of *us*.

Not one of *them*.

November 1787

I'm going to be married; it's settled.

They say we will be — Will and I — the first couple spliced when the pairing off begins at Botany Bay. He's agreeable to it; I've spoken to him.

Now we are leaving behind the Cape of Good Hope.

It took all the courage I had to meet his gaze and break silence — me with hungry-eyed persistence following him about whilst we were putting pitch into cracks on deck. I had Charlotte at my breast the whole time and was thereby excused from heavy work and the burden of chains. Will wouldn't meet my eyes.

He avoided me. I pursued him like a hunting hound. Finally he stopped his pitching duty and gave me back a stare, deep and melancholy and full of foreboding. Then he burst out laughing. Young he was, but the degradation of transportation had aged him. He was my age, twenty-one, if I recalled. Yet his face showed four score and one. I hadn't seen my face in a glass these many months — what creature should greet me there I had no proper notion. An aged crone? I wept to think of it.

Now, Will Bryant was the elected person who handed out the ship's stores to each and every one of us. This responsibility he took with great seriousness, and it had, I think, wrinkled his brow more than Time itself. How he struggled with the exact apportionments — this bit of beef, that measure of grog, this peel of lime, that rind of orange, and so on and so forth. He was a good one, that Will. I saw it in his face when he did the disbursement, so rigorous and careful to be fair that, as a result, each and all trusted him as if he were kin, which, in truth, he felt he was.

Such a man I could love — if there was yet some love in me.

I said to him whilst he was filling a sack with grain on the gray foggy deck that day — just blurted it out with no pre-amble at all — "Would you, Will Bryant, be married to me when we get to Botany Bay?"

He kept his eyes on the sack and said, "Do you need a dress?"

This threw me, and I answered, "I've naught but what I wear, but 'tis good enough."

He grinned, and said, "I mean, lass, there's this sacking here, that, when I'm finished with the dispensing, you could have as your own."

That was his way; and that was his answer.

Yet I knew not if this was my wedding dress . . . it might be, it mightn't be, I had no way of knowing, but I thanked him, anyway, for his kindness. He grew serious then, and asked me to open my palm. Into it he ladled a small little cone of golden grain. "There," he said. "That binds it."

It was something a farm lad might do, not a fisherman from the sea. But he knew naught of farming, and did only what came to him at the moment. My hand closed on that portion of grain as if it were a precious silver ring. I vowed to hold it for all of the voyage, and then some, if I could.

January 1788

Almost to Van Dieman's Land, the *Charlotte* got stuck in a sudden violent gale. It was unsafe to be anywhere but tween decks, as the sea threatened to sink us. All of us women were down on bended knee, praying for deliverance.

I peeked through the slit and saw such a fury. Caught in a white lashing roar, the *Charlotte* was in desperate trouble. The poor beasts above decks were hollering and baying and crying. This, to my way of thinking, was their form of prayer.

Mary Haydon was sick as a dog. And Catherine, too. Little Charlotte was at my breast and bundled in the sackcloth dress I was sewing for my wedding. She was so innocent. What did she know of suffering? What did she know of sinking ships and angry gales?

Well, we weathered it out and finally got to safe harbor. The coast looked unfriendly and cold: The air chilled with fog, the land moorish and dull. How close we were to Botany Bay, we had no way of knowing . . . us prisoners, I mean.

We arrived at Botany Bay and its port called Jackson. But what we saw was not pleasing to the eye, not at first glance — it was cheerless, grassless, and spread out with strange tall, leaf-dripping trees. They looked sorrowful, like naked figures crying in the rain. The odd smell given off by them wasn't unpleasant, however. Mary Haydon said nothing when we came in. She was still too seasick to raise her head. I told her what news we had, that the land smelled good, even though it looked harsh and wild.

Lying on her side, she asked, "Do you see any savages out there?"

I squinted through the slit at the landing. "Some natives, yes."

"Naked?" Mary asked.

"Mostly."

"They seem all right that way," Catherine put in.

"How so?" questioned Mary Haydon.

"Well, they're savages, ain't they?"

Said I to this — "Well, naked or not, they're presently making friends with some of our marines."

However, the natives weren't so friendly among themselves. One afternoon some days later, as we were still confined and provisions were yet being unloaded by our men, we happened to see a great battle right there on the shore. That evening Captain Phillip announced that he was naming the port Manly Cove to commemorate the bravery he had seen that day.

Afterward, he named the place Sydney, but it was forever called Botany Bay by the rest of us.

All the men were off the *Charlotte,* working, making a beginning for us who would, we imagined, be here for all eternity. I was not of that mind, but I hadn't any choice but to accept our fate. So we watched the male prisoners haul cases of saws and make seine poles for fishing and clear the harbor for a camping site, when, all of a sudden, Captain Phillip said, "We shall not be here at all."

The order was then given to bring all the gear back on board. The captain announced that our permanent settlement was to be nine miles northward. There, said he, the hills fairly rolled with flowering trees and the land was like Eden, and all would be well there — which we in our chains doubted most heartily.

As it happened, he was partly right. While it hardly seemed a paradise, the site he had chosen was at the head of the cove on the lush larboard arm of the bay, an area full of inlets, which meant fresh fish, of both sweet and salt. Our men had already started to raise shelters and tents on the west side of the largest stream. On the opposite shore Captain Phillip, who called himself Governor Phillip, began to install himself and his encampment. Still, no women were allowed out of bondage yet; we were all on board the *Charlotte,* waiting. Most of us washed clothes, and I washed my hair for the first time in many months. The wounds inflicted by nits made me sorry for the dousing, but in the afternoon sunshine the sores had already started to heal.

The Landing

Mid-February 1788

🚢 While the men were at work felling trees and erecting huts and putting up tents, we women were finally permitted to disembark. The marines ferried ten or more of us at a time all day, along with bawling livestock and huge sacks of seeds and plants that were laid up along the riverbank.

Altogether we had four mares, two stallions, four cows, one bull, one bull calf, a few sheep, some poultry, goats, and hogs.

We'd started out with 675 people. Of these, forty-eight died on the voyage: forty convicts, five children belonging to them, one marine, the wife of a marine, and a marine's child. And now we were working toward the same goal: build a town on the coast to make a new life.

I couldn't afford to dwell on how much I wanted to leave Port Jackson. But having gotten there, I was already itching to be gone. England was my home, it always would be. Nonetheless, where there was work to be done, I would do it . . . and I wouldn't complain. What a relief, I must say, to be off the *Charlotte* after eight horrible months and some fifteen thousand miles at sea.

So there we were — the fortunate ones, the survivors. Will was a fisherman by trade and thus in this unproven place, he was given the job of provisions-keeper. This meant he had to ensure food for the whole colony. This he could do — given line and net and the right men to haul in the fish. No one knew the sea better than Will.

He came up to me as soon as I got out of the dinghy that first day.

"You won't believe the deal I've struck with Governor Phillip," he said, lowering his voice so none would hear.

I gave him a questioning look.

"Well, Mary Broad, listen you to this. The governor's offered me a position: I'm to be fisherman for the whole colony!"

"Loaves and fishes?" I queried.

"I shall not make manna from heaven," he joked. "But I can provide fishes from the sea — if I've enough nets and line."

"I saw them on the ship in good supply. But that sounds like a lot of work for one man, Will."

He smiled. "I'll have plenty of help."

All at once — in spite of his cheer — I felt a feeling of lostness come over me. After all those months of privation, I found myself on solid ground for the first time . . . and yet I still felt at sea. In truth, I hadn't stopped moving; my body was still floating somewhere on the main.

"Mary," Will said eagerly, taking me gently by the

shoulders. "Do you not see what we have here? The governor has promised us our own private hut — ours!"

"And no one shall share it with us?"

"Just us — you, me, and little Charlotte."

I was taken aback. "He said this, the governor did?"

Will smiled, nodded. "Wake up, girl," he admonished. "It's all to the good."

I looked around me. The seasicky feeling was starting to ebb over slowly, but the land lay long and open and strange to my eye, and it didn't beckon but seemed to say, "Go away."

Then Will's arm came around me. He held me close to him. I glanced at Charlotte, and she smiled.

"We'll be married Sunday next," Will said. "Our new life together will begin then." His eyes were so bright that I wanted to believe he was right and that things had finally turned in our favor, and that our hard luck was soon to run high.

Yet somewhere, deep down inside me, I heard a voice say, "Home is not here."

That night as darkness fell, we sat around a hundred campfires. It was there and then that I got a sudden feeling that some terrible thing was going to happen.

First, I noticed that the fowls all took a high perch upon

the branches of the surrounding trees. Well, that wasn't so unusual, but at home in Fowey, high-roosting fowls meant one thing: A storm was coming. The sky was already dark. The wind was low, and the air was still. It seemed a perfect summer night, yet no stars were present.

It came of a sudden — powerful and unexpected.

Even before the tents could be properly stationed, there came a cold wind, strange and ill boding. It blew through the leaves of the trees so that their undersides turned up, white and pale. Next came lightning and thunder such as I'd never dreamed of seeing or hearing.

Will had tented us on high ground, but he'd only barely driven the pegs into the ground when the blast of wind hit us. The fires winked out, scattering sparks across the night. Tents galloped past like frightened mares.

"Lie yourself down, my birds," said Will in his calmest way. Then he prepared for the worst by going out into the roar of it and trying to tie our tent to an oak tree. This done, he stood guard at the door of the tent, leaving it open so the wind, as he explained, could pass a little through.

"Those tents you see a-blowing off were too tightly fastened," he said, standing guard. Little Charlotte cried. The sudden bursts of noise got her affrighted all the more. So I pressed her to my chest and gently stifled her tears whilst the rain came crashing.

We heard then a terrible clamor, not of weather only but of women crying out in terror.

"What goes?" said I to Will.

He shook his head and took up his wooden pegging-mallet. "Use it I will, if use it I must," he vowed. From where I crouched, whenever the lightning lit up the dark, I saw men running after women.

I shuddered to think of it — my two best friends, Catherine and Mary Haydon, were out there! Hale and hearty Catherine had her marine by her side, but who knows what turn he took?

Thus we passed the hours listening to the storm. After a time the rain and lightning lessened, but the human cries of alarm continued through the terrible long night. Morning dawned. Women sat in rags of despair, shivering in rain-pools of rusty looking water. There were some two hundred unfortunates. All lying about like scattered leaves.

I wept for the sadness of it all.

I looked everywhere — for Catherine or Mary Haydon. Where were they? I asked for them, but no one knew aught of them. And I kept on, carrying little Charlotte, picking my way through the mess of torn tents and strewn belongings. I discovered that no one had died, but many had suffered. Between nature's fury and the fury of the men, prisoners and mariners alike, there were a great many sufferers — all of them women. Those of us who had been spared lent a hand of comfort to the others.

As the day progressed, Governor Phillip called a meeting.

Governor Phillip, no less brassy than always, was uniformed and crisp. He carried a short whip with which he underscored his words by gently smacking his open palm.

"Prisoners," he began, "I've given you a very fair trial on the passage out." He paused to let this sink in. Then went on: "I've had some of you working under my own eye, and I'm sorry to say that most of you are incorrigible, case-hardened rogues fit only for the gallows. After last night, nothing short of death befits your bestial actions."

He hesitated while his eyes drove like nails into the yawning faces of the men.

"If such a scene as last night is ever repeated," he continued, "I shan't bother to try a single one of you. Indeed, I'll have you executed."

Here he flicked the little whip several times and his eyes traveled relentlessly through the hangdog crowd of slack-jawed males who were still yawning and rubbing the sleep from their eyes. It was understood by all of the women what he meant: During the storm some of the rowdiest fellows had roamed like rampant wolves. No effort was made to stop them.

Governor Phillip went on. "You who steal food shall also be put to death. No questions asked; no answers given."

Again, the empty-faced convicts stared glumly out of red-rimmed eyes, and gave nary a nod.

He continued: "You are all expected to work, and work hard. We've lost much through your desertion of duty last night. So many animals swept off to sea. Some may show up yet, but most are gone. We lost tents and lumber."

He paced back and forth while he spoke. Finally, he raised his chin and squared off, as if with every man. "Fortunately," he said, "we lost no munitions. We've enough lead bullets to shoot every one of you."

He roved the rowdy crew with his hawk's eye.

Secretly, I wondered — Why didn't his judicious look ever fall upon his own men? Didn't he know the truth? I'd seen them raping and pillaging with the best of the worst. Yet the governor gave the uniformed rapists no glance whatsoever.

When this indictment and warning was done, we broke into rank and file and marched back to the governor's, calling, "God save the king," and a return chorus from the convicts of the same.

Then the marines fired shots into the air three times and we went back to trying to rebuild what was so badly broken down — the whole of our pitiful camp.

As fate would have it, I found Catherine and Mary Haydon, alive and well. They were both hiding in a cave down by the river-mouth. At the first outbreak of the storm, they'd gotten together and run along the coast. They were seafaring Cornwall girls and they knew how to hide from a storm. They heard the madness of the men and the shrieks of the women. But they thought it was all on account of the rain and the lightning. Safe and dry, they stayed holed up until well after Governor Phillip's reprimand.

"I got some sleep, anyway," said Catherine.

"I — no worse," Mary Haydon said. "And where was you, Mary Broad?" she wanted to know.

"Will and I were in our tent when the violence broke out. Surely you heard the women being attacked?"

They gazed strangely at me.

"Was it not the storm then?" Catherine queried.

"There was that — and much worse," I told them.

They asked to know more, so I went on about the whole rotten affair of deviltry. When I was through, Catherine shook her head. "The Lord above has watched over His children, Catherine and Mary, in their time of need."

To which I concurred. But what of the others? The broken ones? Where was the Lord looking then?

Late February 1788

Sailors say, "When there is a storm, there must follow a calm."

That was what happened after the dread and terrible night.

Things calmed down considerably. Still, sickness increased. Mostly dysentery and scurvy. The former we treated with the red gum of a local tree. This was shown to us by one of the natives. The work of every able-bodied man and woman was clearing the ground and erecting the camp. To a great extent, the intensity of such work calmed the nerves and settled the soul. There was no room for drowsiness, or churlishness, with so much to do. The marines and sailors were punished with utmost severity for even trivial offenses, so they were most constantly on guard. This — and the convicts' better behavior — seemed to mollify the fears of the women after that deviltry night.

Soon after came that special day when the Reverend Richard Johnson held a service under the tree of oak at the top of the hill overlooking our camp.

Our wedding day had arrived.

I was in such great straits that day — though I shouldn't

have been. The life of a married person was better by far in that colony; and Will and I knew this full well.

When the time came I wore my sackcloth dress over the fresh-washed shirt given me by Mr. Tench. Will wore the same pair of frayed trousers he'd had on in Portsmouth. But his hair, brown and full of curls, I'd washed with lye soap, so it was clean. His pewter-colored eyes gleamed — so I thought, anyway.

Catherine and Mary Haydon stood by, as bridesmaids. Each one carried a bouquet of flowers that resembled English roses; yet they had no smell. Will's best man was a green-eyed, handsome friend from County Antrim, Ireland. A thiever of lead, his record said, but a more honest fellow you couldn't have found. James Martin was convicted and sentenced the same time I was, so I'd known him a good little while.

Governor Phillip said a few words to the reverend, and the ceremony began quite promptly. Alongside us were five other couples to be joined in matrimony. Peeking down the row, I felt a sense of glad tidings. Not only this, but the sun was shining and people were smiling.

Forthwith, Governor Phillip bade us step closer to him. Then he made the following pronouncement: "You Bryant, and you, Mary Broad, shall be the first couple married in the settlement." He let this sink in for a moment while he cleared his throat. He raised his chin and looked upon the convicts seated on the ground. No one said anything, nor was there any murmur to be heard. Just silence. Some far-off crows cackled, then a greater silence.

I was exceedingly nervous. I blushed myself red in the face. My palms dampened. Will's hand was almost sticky in mine. But for his part, he remained true to form, standing tall. He neither smiled nor frowned, but kept a still, small mouth.

The night before, he'd told me the wedding, as such, would mean nothing in England — "Why, it's not even legally binding, Mary," he said.

Said I, "But it's all we've got."

"Don't worry. I'll keep my end of the bargain until that time both of us shall leave this colony for good."

"You still love me, don't you?"

But he never replied, which was hurtful to me.

Yet there we were the next day, about to be married, committed by colony law to a life together. At the same time, we were equally committed to a partnership of escape. If marriage was the door to that, Will wanted to walk through it. I felt someways different, I confess. I believe I loved him, in spite of what he'd said to me.

Governor Phillip went on with the ceremony.

"Smugglers and thieves though you be, today you shall make a fresh start. Now, Mr. Johnson, go ahead and splice them."

So the reverend read through his service after which Governor Phillip slipped off one of his finger rings. He passed it to the reverend, who lent it to us. This little ring went the rounds for each of the couples until, well spent, it slipped back onto the governor's finger.

Sometimes I wish there were more to the wedding than I speak of now — but it wasn't so. We were married faster than the secret snare trips the life of a partridge.

Someone made a joke about the ring, which everyone heard.

One of the marines said, "They're more landlocked than wedlocked."

The laughs went around at our expense. Well, the reverend pretended he didn't like it one bit. He said right loud — "Listen, men, you should try to remember that even *these people* have feelings, so keep your thoughts to yourselves and say no more." But he said this with a smile and a wink of the eye.

Mr. Tench was in amongst the marines. I glanced quickly at him; he stared stiffly ahead. He kept looking off toward the sea, as if he wished himself far away. All in all, no one had done more to keep me alive than Tench. I owed him that, and this marriage, too, for that matter. Let no one say he wasn't a fair enough fellow.

So I was Mary Broad no more. My maids-at-hand, Catherine and Mary Haydon, hugged me and kissed me — and, a little reluctantly, Will did, too — and I was, from then on, Mary Bryant, and the weakness I'd felt starting out went swiftly away, and we signed the register. Well, I put my X on the line, for at that time I could no way make my signature or even scrawl my initial.

And it was done, and done indeed, on Botany Bay.

In our tent that night, Will turned in his sleep and, without waking, mumbled, "We're no criminals."

The Colony

October 1788

The squally, rainy months had passed. A young man, barely more than a boy, was hanged for stealing bread and sugar from the store tent. Though a mere youth, this boy Bennett was considered by the mariners to be a "hardened old offender." Sadly, he started his offenses at the age of eleven by stealing a watch, a steel chain, a key, a hook, and two shirts. Before dying, he said, "I apologize for living so wicked a life."

The marines say that we're a miserable lot — all of us. That we deserve to live in the squalor of this wicked camp. That, like Bennett, we will, sooner or later, find ourselves at the end of a noose.

Last night, this marine crept into a woman prisoner's tent and attacked her. She screamed loudly; more marines came. They caught the man and took him to Governor Phillip. This is one of the first times that justice was served out to those who justly deserved it. The man received 150 lashes for his deeds. But I have a feeling he was no favorite of the governor.

The great and main difficulty is that the mariners — save their uniform — were no better than criminals themselves. Yet they erected a gallows and triangles to remind us that *we're* the ones to blame for all that went sour in that colony. The gallows stood on a little knoll. I noticed that it was the roost of black, croaking jackdaws like back in England. It gave me the shivers to see them and their haunted hangout where so many men died.

The triangle was made by tying logs together so that, in the middle of them, a man or a woman could be strung out — arms and legs held forcefully and painfully apart. On this cruel device, convicts were beaten, hung out, and left to dry.

A glance away from this evil field and its grim reminders of our fate was our little village of tents and huts, firestones and kitchens. I own that the worst of these huts was so flimsy that a puff of wind often brought it down. Few prisoners had training in the building trades. In fact, there were but twelve in the camp of hundreds who could make anything that stood up properly.

To put an honest face on things, we were good and lost. Most of us came from towns where the gulling of standard citizens was a kind of occupation. Truthfully, some of these ragmen and tatterwomen squatting before their cook fires with soot-smudged cheeks were once the pick of the litter, moving serenely about the crowds at Piccadilly Square, fleecing the unwary and the slow of foot.

Such was the life of a lucky thief.

Yet now they were trying to steal crumbs from a cruel place that, day by day, bore down on them. The heat was one thing, the marines another. All the little convict gardens were flopped over, the seedlings dying from lack of water and protection.

What chance did these men have of becoming farmers?

Governor Phillip was always ordering them to haul firewood or press bricks and such. So none had time for personal matters — no moment to spare for real needs . . . just work.

The comforts fell to the marines; the forced labor to the convicts.

One morning while mending a fishing net, Will said to me, "It comes hard upon my spirit the way these city people struggle so to bait a hook, pull a line, or throw a net. I don't think we have a single fisherman in the lot except William Allen. But, my God, he's an old man."

"What of James Martin? He's always helping around."

"With his tongue — giving advice. Oh, he's a great help, Mary, but certainly no man of the sea, sad to say."

I then asked him about Nathaniel Lilley, who was often seen lending a hand where it was needed.

"Aye," said Will, "there's a perky little man, to be sure. But he's weak for such hard labor. Sam Broom's strong as an ox, but . . ."

"What?"

". . . cantankerous as a crab, as well."

"We should cook him, then," I offered. To which he gave a small laugh, and shook his head.

"'Tis all but *hopeless*."

"We'll have to make it *hopeful,* then," I advised.

I sympathized with him, however, for I knew well that, even being a woman, I was better off at working than most of the men. Even I could see when the mullet ran, and chiefly what they were, and moreover how to prepare them for a meal. We were eating fish quite regular now — a horse mackerel was boiled up by me the other night, and it tasted of home. We had cod, skipjack, and even a delicious swordfish. Such eatings were not available in Fowey — not so close to shore, anyway.

"I know," Will said, "that these people haven't eyes in their heads for this sort of thing — fishing. But they could try harder, for it's only when we work as a whole that each man gets a better life for himself."

"They're still sweet on gulling and thieving," said I, and I knew it to be true.

He was straightening some of the homemade hooks that he rigorously cleaned and baited, and readied for each day's fishing out in the bay.

"Why are they bent so?" I asked him.

He frowned. "The sharks are fearsome. Have you not seen it?"

"I allow as to how I've seen their fins, coming and going, yes."

"Haven't you seen the bull sharks, Mary? They'll take a mullet off your line, along with your hand — if you let them. I've seen them go crunching up the sand beach to get a runaway bonita. You must've cast an eye that way, and seen it yourself."

I admitted it. But sharks weren't something strange to us who lived by the sea. I mentioned that to Will, and he said these sharks were quite different.

"Is that why *all* the hooks look so?"

"In the mouth of one of these bulls a hook's but a wee little fishbone."

Will looked more discouraged than I'd ever seen him in some weeks. It wasn't the fishing, I supposed, but rather the men he went a-fishing with.

"You mustn't give in, Will. You've got to keep your spirits up. Without you, the whole camp would die. Even the hunters aren't fit to bring back enough meat. It's the fish we depend on."

"It's rubbish, Mary, you know that. Why, the rogues hardly eat of the fish I catch. They want meat, they say. These

London rats don't bide with fishy flesh — they want bloody meat. Animals are all they want."

I began now to see an end of Botany Bay Colony — and it frightened me. What held us aright was hope. But we had little of it to go around, and so many of the convicts chose not to work — not for themselves or for anyone else. When forced, they made bricks. When left alone, they filched and gambled and stole from one another. Governor Phillip's rule of "No work, no food," was always turned awry by men with a clever eye for thieving goods that didn't belong to them. This would undermine us, in the end, I knew. For when there were no more things to take, the desperate would grow even more desperate.

Cannibalism was sometimes brought up among the men of Botany Bay. People spoke of it — in jest, of course.

"I tell you, Will," I said, handing him his mended net. "Fish for us, then. Don't worry about the rabble. They'll eat or not eat, but we must, on account of little Charlotte, stay alive."

"To escape," he added, his eyes brightening a little.

"We shall, Will. We shall escape. You know the time will come. And when it does, we'll be the only ones prepared to take the chance."

🐜   🐜   🐜

As time went on, and the weeks turned into months, hunger was stamped on every face. And yet the fish was there; they just didn't want it. Rations of old salted meat, dried peas, and weevily flour were cut to a very spare allowance. Not near enough to keep a man alive, and women got two-thirds less than the men, and children even less than that.

In addition to hunger, there were other fearsome odds against us. Smallpox and scurvy were now in the thick of the camp. People were dying every day of known diseases, and some new ones that we knew naught of. Children suffered from quick midnight fevers. By morning, they were gone. By noon, buried. After that, no more was said of them, as if mourning would bring more bad luck.

Fear was in all the faces now, etched deep. And it grew like a dark and dreadful blossom around the camp, so that the smell of death and the sound of it were a flower of evil that spoke to us in our sleep.

I kept my hands full with the salting and smoking of mullet and bream, horse mackerel, skate, and rock cod, of which we — Will and little Charlotte and I — ate and thus grew strong in the sight of ever-present death. Sometimes, Mary Haydon and Catherine joined us, but I saw less and less of them. They each had found marines of their own, and these men did not like to see them with the likes of us. This hurt me sorely, as they were like sisters to me.

We wondered, Will and I, if our luck could last; it seemed too good to be true that we had food and shelter. By then, so many months after our arrival at Port Jackson, we were living in the place called Farm Cove. This was well away from the main camp, far from the prying eyes of the miserable masses, huddled by their smoking fires and emptying their nasty necessary buckets too close to their dwellings.

Indeed, I saw one man throwing excrement in the river, the place where people drink! And, in the foulness of rain and heat and cold and murderous insects, the stench rose and cast a mortifying blow on all who tried to live there. Thank the Lord, we lived apart!

Well, as long as we kept catching and supplying fish, we were considered valuable to the colony. Enough of the marines ate fish to keep us in good stead with the governor; indeed, he, too, was a fish-eater. Yet I feared for our lives, as a new danger had just arisen.

We were deemed *privileged*. Which is to say, we had a hut of our own and we lived alone in it; and in our camp, anyway, hunger and death were not prowling. This made for jealousy. And there were those who believed we ought to be stripped of our house and the cutter we fished in. There were folk so mean, they snuck around at night, seeking to find anything we might leave out that could be of use to them.

One night, Will caught a thief dragging off our cast-iron

pot. He struck the purloiner on the head with his mallet, and the man dropped softly in the sand. It was one of the fishermen Will worked with every day, a fellow he trusted.

"Will you report him?" I asked, holding little Charlotte and standing in the cold starlight.

Will shook his head.

"If I do, he'll do worse."

"Or someone else will."

He nodded.

The man crawled off, slithering like a snake.

Another night, when I was up feeding Charlotte and slapping mosquitoes, I heard the crunching teeth of the bull sharks as they ran fish up on the beach. They devoured them, fully half out of the water, in full view of the moon.

The sound of those gnashing teeth were with me for many nights following, though the sharks themselves, for some reason, stayed out by the reef.

January 1789

Mr. Tench, who was away at Norfolk Island Colony for six months, had returned to our camp to see how we'd fared. It touched my heart to see him. He'd grown heavier apace, perhaps from living on that other colony. Word had it they had a longer growing season and conditions withal that were better off than ours. In any case, Mr. Tench brought us a little gift of wrapped Norfolk pork, which I fell upon to frying at once.

Lighting his pipe, he shook his head. "I'm so sorry, Mary, to see the condition of the people here."

"They're all but starved," said Will bitterly.

"The supply ships never showed," Mr. Tench added. "The *Sirius* has gone off for help, but she won't be back for months. Meanwhile —"

"Meanwhile, we'll starve," Will interrupted.

Mr. Tench drew judiciously on his pipe, yet said no more. But for his soiled uniform and missing buttons, he looked much the same.

"Are you not still providing fish for the camp, Will?" he asked.

"I fish for all, but keep no extra for us anymore — that's the new law, in case you haven't heard."

"A cruel one it is," said I. The governor had imposed it, we knew, because of other convicts' envy of our position.

"Is the baby all right?"

"She sleeps."

"Has she enough to eat?"

"I sifted the sand for some spillage of meal to make our porridge this morning. It goes hard with her, as it does for all of us. They're dying for want of food in the main camp."

He saw the pain in my eyes, and replied softly, "You durst not say it came from my mouth — hold back some fish for yourselves. That's my advice."

Will thrust out his chin, his brow dark under his shaggy head of hair. "Do you know the penalty for keeping back a single fish?"

"Lashes?"

"Death."

Mr. Tench sighed. "Have any men been treated so?" he asked, tapping his pipe against a stone.

"Your marines," said Will, "have flogged men for less. Yesterday, I saw a man tied with hands behind his back and banished into the wilderness."

Mr. Tench raised his eyebrows.

"For what?"

"For telling a tale about finding gold."

"He did *that,* and no more?"

"That, and no more."

"We're lost . . . the colony's lost," I told him.

Then, for a long time, while the fragrance of the frying pork filled the air with its wondrous smell, the three of us remained quiet. Every so often I glanced over my shoulder to see if some stray noise was what I imagined it to be — an attack of some kind, either from a marine or a convict. Even with Mr. Tench present, I felt unsafe.

At last, Mr. Tench spoke. He rubbed his chin, as I'd seen him do onboard ship. He drew himself up and stood before the fire. "You two are survivors," he said. "Do you know any natives?"

"Well, I've seen their shadows on the edge of the trees to the west of us. They never appear in numbers, just a few at a time."

"If I were you, I'd make a friend or two. It can't hurt; those folk know all there is to know about this strange land of theirs."

He tamped and lit his pipe. Then added, "I've a friend that I made before going to Norfolk. Name's Arabanoo. Don't know whither he's gone, or if he still lives, but if he does, I shall send him to you. Maybe he can provide you with some native food, or the way to snare it. They're awfully clever with traps and things."

"Your kindness," I told him, "is most gratefully received. Without you . . ." Here I stopped, unable to continue.

That night we ate like kings and queens of times gone by, and the next day like magic, Arabanoo showed up, and he stayed with us for quite some time, showing us many things.

Unfortunately, Arabanoo wasn't a well man. He, like others of his tribe, had contracted a sickly cough from the convict camp. For this reason, I feared his being there almost as much as I feared his not being there.

Nonetheless, he explained how to make a stone-painted spear and how to roast roots in an underground oven. He taught us how to catch the large possums that lived in the meadows. He taught me how to make clothing out of thin shreds of papery bark, and how to boil water in a rock cleft by building a fire around it. Will and I grew wise in Arabanoo's company. His friendliness was a sign of hope, beside which we kindled the dream of our escape.

One morning Will was summoned and brought before the judge advocate. Some dark and evil things were swiftly proved upon him. The main charge was stealing fish. This went hard on him, and his sentence was rumored to be death by hanging.

Although I wanted to throw myself down and vent my tears, I did no such thing. I firmly resolved to see Will's sentence commuted. Thus I took little Charlotte in my arms and I went to Governor Phillip.

He met me in front of his quarters, a wooden building, the only real house in the colony. The sun was shining brightly on the front windows of his house, and I saw that he had potted some yellow flowers in each window casement.

"Sir," I spoke out, meeting him head-on, "I confess my husband's indiscretion. But his small weakness was acted out because of our baby. As he is the provider of fish for the entire colony, you must concede that his punishment is too harsh. You can't kill your only fisherman, sir."

Charlotte stirred and cried all the while I spoke. The governor looked on with a face of calm indifference. He betrayed no feeling one way or the other. Behind his gold-capped shoulders and bright uniform, the sunlight streamed off his cut-glass windows.

When I finished talking, I looked straight at him, but he moved not a muscle. His face, so stern and implacable, might have been made of carver's leather.

He frightened me, I must say — not by his speech but by his silence.

Finally, he shrugged. The look of indifference didn't change. Nor did his stiff posture. I glanced at his leggings, his broadcloth coat, and wondered if he wasn't roasting inside them, as I was sweating plenty where I stood in the hot sun.

"I shall speak to the judge advocate, Mary Bryant," he told me so very casually, almost as if he were saying, "I'm going for a drink of water."

Yet, in the end, it wasn't all that he did. His flinty mind saw the truth of my words, and by day's end the trial was held in view of the triangles and gallows' pole.

The judge advocate was a narrow-headed man by the name of David Collins, who was, after all this time, softhanded and white of face — as if he'd never been out in the sun or seen a day of work. There was another man, too, who proved himself our worst enemy. This was Joseph Paget. Nasty he was from all the way back to the *Dunkirk*. But now he proved himself a Judas, as well.

When I look narrowly upon it, I must admit that Mr. Paget was, in some way, paid to say what he did.

"I warrant," said he, whose thick-lipped stuttering was always laughed at by all, "that this-this-this Will Bryant has been leeching fish . . . off the colony all along. I was be-seeched by him and his fellow fisherman to sell their catch on the sly."

At this, a rumble of voices arose.

John White, the surgeon who delivered Charlotte, stepped up briskly and said, "I find this quite hard to believe. I've known Will Bryant since the *Dunkirk.* I have found him to be strictly honest in all of his dealings with me. Only if his family were starving, which I judge to be the case, might he deviate from the strictest rule of the law."

So saying, he stepped back and glared menacingly at Paget, who crept into his crowd of ruffians and hunkered out of sight.

Governor Phillip raised his chin and looked around the sea of dismal faces. His keen eyes searched for me and rested there. Then he glanced at Will, who stood quite apart, his hands chained behind his back. His head was bent down and his eyes seemed fixed upon his feet.

I mention this because just at that moment, the gover-nor's eye lit on the judge advocate's, and I saw a flicker of something pass between these two men. Will, however, saw nothing of this exchange.

Then the sentence was read by the judge advocate.

"We hereby find Will Bryant guilty. We sentence him to receive one hundred lashes, and to be deprived of the direction of fish and boat, and to be turned out of the hut he is now in, along with his family."

My mind went blank. I trained my eyes on my poor husband. He was taken off to the triangle, and duly beaten, without a moment being wasted.

In truth, there was no time for reflection on any account. My heart was beating fast, and my head was reeling.

Just like that — we were cast out!

We were outcasts in a society of outcasts.

There was naught I could do but stand and watch and feel every biting whip-crack as if it were my own. The tears blinded me, but I stayed, unmoving, for the hundredth lash. All the while, Charlotte screamed. I couldn't find any way to still her or comfort her. Finally an old and familiar face appeared — Catherine.

She took Charlotte with her off to one side of the sentencing field, and I knew my little girl was in good hands. At the same time, James Martin, Will's best man, and Nathaniel Lilley, both kindhearted fellows from our fishing crew, came toward me and patted me on the back. When I felt my legs going soft, it was these two who held me up.

Afterward, two marines dragged Will off, unconscious. They took him to a stockade by the governor's house. The grumbling, shiftless crowd dispersed reluctantly, still hungry for violence.

Mary Haydon appeared then. She had some cloths, clean water, and salt.

"Thank you," I said when I finally found my voice.

We were allowed, Mary Haydon and I, to enter the stockade and tend to Will. But marine guards watched over us the whole time we were there. With each rub of salt, Will let out a little sigh. He stiffened with the pain. There was no other way to purify the wounds, but it hurt me to do it.

As I looked at my poor husband's torn skin, I vowed to escape Botany Bay soon — or die trying.

April 1789

🚢 Our new home was not anything like our old one by the sea. We now were quartered in a big, stuffy barracks where the male and female convicts took up their dismal, yet separate residences. Amidst the flotsam and jetsam of so many people, we squatted and made ourselves to home in a stench of unwashed bodies and unmerciful heat.

It was a shock to lie down on the hard ground when we'd been so used to soft sand. Worse — there were rivers of ants everywhere, running about. Wherever we turned, they swarmed. Too, in the low, moist, ill-smelling air, the mosquitoes hung in clouds around our heads. Their whining evil was always in our ears.

Each morning we discovered our skin was all bumpy from the bites. Charlotte was constantly pulling at her cheeks, crying out in discomfort. Yet what could I do? Some of us actually took a native cure for this pestilence — mud. And packed it all over our faces and arms before going to sleep. It was effective, but, as you can imagine, uncomfortable . . . and dreadful hot, like a mask!

One night I woke to a disturbing cry. I thought it was Charlotte. However, she was sleeping well enough. I got up and crept over the sleeping bodies to the open door of the barracks. There — not ten feet from where I stood — a huge yellowish snake was crushing and devouring a frog. With each tightening of those pitiless coils, the white frog uttered a cry like the bleating of a child.

Disgusted, I turned to my pallet and went back to sleep. But I fell into nightmares of beasts until I wakened, all of a-sweat and my heart pounding in fear. The cry of that hapless frog was still in my thoughts.

Will was never the same after that beating. When I greeted him each morning, he merely nodded, tugging on his clothes glumly. The weeks dragged by in miserable fashion. Without means to fish, we ate like rats. No, the truth is, we actually ate rats — of the variety that lived in trees. Under the circumstances, they were passable fare.

With each day, I longed for our little private house by the seaside sand. With each week, I prayed for the return of Will Bryant, for it was as if a stranger had inhabited his beaten, defeated body. This new Will never spoke of escape; indeed, never talked at all. His eyes stared emptily ahead, and when I said his name, I had to say it thrice before he acknowledged me.

Long before Will's back had begun to heal, he was marched off to dig clay to make bricks for Governor Phillip's town. At night when Will returned, his face was frozen in a frown. There was a streak of white in the hair at his temples that seemed to have come in a single night. Verily, he looked older than he was, much older.

One day, while lacing his boot, he said to me, "Mary, how much more will you take of this?"

"How much longer — will — I?"

I was working then in the lime kiln yard, making lime for the clay roofing tiles of the governor's make-believe mansions. My hands were blistered and cracked. Always, my eyes stung from the dry lime dust. My mouth was full of its bitter flavor. I coughed endlessly in the night.

"What will it be, Mary?" Will continued.

His eyes looked awake for the first time in weeks.

"We have no means to do anything," I said dejectedly. "Except what they make us do."

"Our luck could change," Will said with some animation. I saw a flicker of rebellion in his eyes.

We said no more at that time. As we knew, only those who wished to die talked of escape. But not only those who escaped died. The death toll mounted each day. Some died in their sleep, but most crumpled to the ground, tool in hand, while the marines stood by, fearing to touch them.

Soon we had streets, if mud-wallows could be called avenues. And houses — if falling-down shacks could be named dwellings. Windows — we had none. Lattices of twigs filled the open casements. But these did little more than keep out the lightest of rains. We had a cemetery — if stick crosses at the end of a row of ramshackle houses could be called a churchyard.

The news came that when a sufficient number of bricks were made, there would be a church, too. Its name was already ordered by the governor: It was to be called Saint Phillip's Church.

Meanwhile, dysentery raged on, and with it, starvation. We ate land crabs — dark, nasty monsters that roamed the camp at night. Our gardens were beaten down, ruined by the rains. The colony's rations seemed to have gone all to the marines. The old people died quietly. The young cried out in anguish. Yet sick or not, we were forced to work at hard labor every day.

One morning, after some days of sopping rain, I looked out of the barracks and saw that all of the paperwood trees were in bright blossom. The pretty pills of white looked like a Christmas snow under skies of blue. Here I thought we'd fallen so low and that death was very near, but on this day as we went along to work, I felt hopeful again. The only thing that troubled me was that I felt stomach-sick most mornings. A familiar feeling, too, and that was what worried me.

Governor Phillip himself met us on our way.

He kept a distance, holding a cloth over his mouth and nose.

"Bryant is needed again for his knowledge of fishing," he said matter-of-factly. "He's necessary, I believe. Why, the whole enterprise is unmanageable without him."

Somehow, hiding his face behind that white handkerchief, he seemed almost spiritlike, like a wraith that had appeared out of the early morning mists.

"Do you mean it?" Will asked.

The governor hesitantly lowered the cloth. "Are you people not sick?"

"We're quite alive, Your Honor," I answered.

He nodded.

"Then get your belongings and go back to your former residence." He paused, then said, "And — Bryant, catch some fish, will you? No one else seems to have a notion how to do it."

In a quickened beat of the heart, there we were — back where we belonged in our old hut by the sea. Nor was this all — the fish were momentarily plentiful, and Will caught great nets of them. Our condition grew better apace. The governor had said, "You have my permission to hold back one fish each day for your own use." So Will made sure that his fish was the largest of the day's catch.

Charlotte threw off her cold, and I stopped coughing, and we went back to eating smoked mullet, as we were wont to do before; and we never tired of this fish.

Nonetheless, though things were some better, we were no less resolved to make our escape. Each day we thought of it, planning our remove, little by little, night by night. The long coast glittered in the flickery starlight, and we saw ourselves upon it, or off to one side of it, floating like the open-winged herons that were always gliding out of our sight into the mysterious north.

My newest and heaviest burden was that I was with child again. My belly swelled. I was often tired. The days crept more slowly for me. To put an honest face on the thing, I thought only of escape, even as the babe grew in my belly. There was never a time when I didn't think of getting away from that godforsaken colony.

The Second Fleet with more prisoners had just arrived, which was why Governor Phillip wanted Will to pursue his fishing again. With hundreds of new mouths to feed, and more illnesses to deal with, and with almost no other supplies, the situation was quite hopeless. No amount of fish could meet the requirements of the whole ravenous camp. Once again, starvation stalked, hollow-eyed and evil.

I should guess there were 350 more people for Will to feed. So he was out from sunrise to sunset. He was faithfully met by James Martin, Nathaniel Lilley, Sam Bird, and James Cox.

They went off with their tattered seiner's nets and the other flagging, unfaithful men, who were there one day and not the next, for none knew aught of fishing, nor cared to acquaint themselves, either.

Will — and those few good men — did the work of a whole navy of fishermen while the others rested on their oars and gossiped about picking pockets by the Thames.

One evening, while I was boiling some fish soup, Will said he'd heard some strange news from one of the new men.

Said Will, "This fellow's recently come from England and says the Third Fleet's due to arrive soon."

He sat thoughtfully on a driftwood bench.

"More mouths to feed," he moaned. Then, looking out at the spangled copper sea, he sighed. "How am I to do it, Mary?"

Then he dropped his head into his hands and I thought I heard him sob.

Charlotte cried at the exact same time. Did she feel his grievous uncertainty? So it seemed to me.

The specter of death peered now out of every crack and, betimes, out of the eyes of innocent children. Even the new-born had the scared look of uncommon fear in its eyes — it was the stock-and-trade of the camp.

Our son, Emmanuel, was born in the dark moon of this

frightful time. He came all of a sudden. My water burst and he was there. It was that quick. Catherine and Mary Haydon helped with the delivery.

He was pretty-eyed, like Will. And his tiny face hadn't the stamp of the hungry, the sick, and forlorn. "There's hope here," I said when I first saw him.

"You daren't call him that," said Catherine.

Mary Haydon added, "If you call him something like hope, can't you make another name for it?"

"I want to call him Emmanuel. Doesn't that mean hope?"

"If it does, he's born to the wrong world."

"But maybe not the wrong time," said Mary Haydon. "Look how easy a birth it was."

"He's my baby. I'll call him any name I like."

"Of course you will, dear," said Catherine.

And I did.

The Plan

Time passed — infants were born and buried on the same day. One man was charged for neglecting work. Another for being drunk. Fifty lashes was the usual sentence. Will Bryant was reprimanded publicly for drunkenness, but he was not flogged. His work was too important for that. Some convicts, going to the woods for greens, were murdered and mutilated by natives. So the governor had put a ban on their visiting us.

By now, I dreamed of escape each night. In my dreams I saw us break free of human tyranny — only to fight against a stronger opponent: Nature. Yet I was willing to face the odds, whatever they were. Anything was better than slowly withering under the lash.

Secretly, Will made friends with Bennelong, the black native, who came often to see our catch. I myself was friends with his wife, whose name I couldn't pronounce, Nganyinytja. Naturally, I shortened it to Ngan.

Though we knew not how to speak their tongue and they avoided trying ours, still our friendship was strong. And it was abetted by gestures of the heart. Bennelong became a good companion for Will and showed him many useful things. Luckily, we lived far off enough not to be watched — or so we thought.

More the better — Charlotte played, innocently and cheerfully, with Bennelong's little girl. All the while I sat and watched them, our newborn, Emmanuel, at my breast.

As the days passed, I witnessed much goodness on the part of these new friends. Bennelong went fishing with Will almost every day. The result was more fish, and of a greater size. The man's skills at spear-fishing were amazing to behold. Snapper and grouper made it to our supper table, and the white meat was good and warmed our bellies.

One afternoon when I had nothing to do, Ngan taught me the way she knew to make bread. This was done from grass seedpods, which were stone-ground and mixed with water to make a paste. The dough was then cooked in the fire ashes. It was a hard bread, more delicious than words can describe. Our whole family relished it.

Will, for his part, was learning the orbs of the night sky. Such teaching of Bennelong was worthwhile, as it explained how these tribesmen could travel great distances across many miles of water. They used the seabirds and the stars like a kind of map.

Bennelong learned a lot from Will, too. He was not — nor had he ever been — a net fisherman. Will taught him how to do this, and he was most grateful. In return, he showed Will even more things about staying alive in the wilderness.

Ngan, on another occasion, showed me how to capture honey ants. They had special "food chiefs," the ants did. These were huge, rather round ants whose bodies were filled with stored honey. You could eat dozens of them. They were so sweet, and the children liked chasing them; though at first, thinking they were evil like the ones at the big camp, they spanked the honey out of them. Smiling, Ngan showed Charlotte how to gently pinch the fat ants and squeeze the honey into her mouth. It became a great game and we enjoyed playing it. All the while, staying alive, a plan grew in us. It was there when we knew not of it.

December 1790

More time went by. One day I met up with Catherine, with whom I hadn't had a good visit since the birth of Emmanuel. She looked the worse for wear, as I am sure I did, but we took up other things to talk about and didn't tarry on our looks.

"Catherine," said I, "there's a new ship in. She's called the *Supply,* and she has, I hear, stores from Batavia."

She smiled wanly. "More food means more mouths will be coming soon — you've heard that, too, I'm sure."

She dropped her eyes to her shoeless feet, and I saw how badly callused and cracked and blackened they were.

"What's that ship anchored behind the *Supply*?" Catherine asked, squinting into the sparks of the sea.

"She's called *Waaksamheyd.*"

Catherine looked at me dubiously.

"I can't even put tongue to that," she said, frowning.

I smiled. "Can't speak for what it means, but Will has learnt the truth of her mission. More food, Catherine. The captain's Dutch, a kindly sort of fellow. He's promised to go back to Batavia and fetch us more goods."

Catherine kept her frown, however. "Little good that'll do the likes of us," she said dryly. "It goes for naught. What the

captains do for good, we undo for bad, if you get my meaning. In camp, there's fights every night. You wouldn't know a
thing of it, living off so fine as you do."

I caught then a trace of her jealousy.

"When Will was punished," I said, "there was enough of
that quarreling and killing going on; believe you me, I saw it
a-plenty. We had our hard times back there, Catherine."

"For the rest of us, they're still going on," she snapped.

"Even with your marines watching over you?"

"They're as faithful as roosters," Catherine replied.

I wished, more than I could say, to tell her of the plan.
But I was sworn to secrecy by my husband.

Anyway, soon after this, Catherine hung her head, and
left.

We parted friends, though I felt a tug at my heart seeing
her so — she was always little-boned, but now she looked
frail and old, and there were wisps of white in her gold hair.

It touched my heart forcibly as I walked the beach to
home, carrying Emmanuel, and the odd thing was Catherine
had never said a word about him or really looked at him
carefully.

As I approached our hut, still feeling Catherine's poverty
hard upon my spirit, I saw Will sitting on a rock talking to a
stranger. The man was wearing a captain's two-cornered hat.
It had been a while since I had seen a wig as clean and neat

as his. From his uniform I could tell he was Dutch. This was all to the good. The Dutch did not hold with our English penal system.

"Mary," Will said, getting up swiftly, "this is Captain Detmer Smith. I've asked him to sup with us, such as it is."

I hadn't seen Will so animated of face in many a long month. He was fairly jumping as he boiled us some tea. The captain, for his part, was surprisingly at ease among us, and I began now to see a certain fondness that he affected for myself.

I felt his eyes on me from the moment I met him. But I own that this bothered me not — after all, he was here, he said, to help us out.

After the portly fellow departed that night, and Will and I lay snug in our sand-smoothed bed, Will started laying out his plan. "This man, Detmer Smith, is our way off this hellish parcel, Mary."

"How so?" I asked.

"Well, food, for one thing."

Will went on, "I can't tell you, Mary, how this raises up my hopes. I tell you, this man likes us mightily — and I scarce know the reason. Why, he's already offered us his aid."

"In *what way*?" I asked suspiciously, remembering the man's eye upon me.

"He's already given me spirits — rum."

"So that's why you're so good-natured, Will."

"I won't say I'm not a little bit aglow from the drink he gave me. But here's why I've put off despair. If we befriend him, he will provide us with all that we need to get away. The man came out and said he doesn't approve of the colony killing off the convicts who build it."

For a time I lay quiet, thinking. But as I came to look more narrowly on this easing of our woes, it seemed to mean something other than Will said it did. I asked him then, "What *befriending* are you speaking of?"

He stammered, "I — I mean only that if it should please you to do more than just take up his clothes for washing and baking bread for him, you —"

I cut him off, as I knew that it was the spirits talking, not Will. I'd occasion to see him like this before — more often, in fact, than I'd want to admit. His breath smelled sour that night, I should say.

Now I turned plainly away from him, giving him the cold shoulder. He did the same, and there was no more talking of our escape. Yet I lay awake, my mind racing like a mill wheel. Was I jeopardizing our future by trying to protect myself?

If so, I would swallow my pride.

I'd done so before, and would do so again.

January 1791

As time went on, I began to see that by helping Detmer Smith, our lives were to be made easier in the main. Quite regular he brought us flour and meat to cook, while he stayed to sit and smoke his pipe, and thence to eat with us. His dark eyes were on me all the while; never a moment were they turned to anything else. But I gave him no easy freedom on that account. Often I acted as his carrier, to and from the ship, and once he waited for me to get belowdecks. While I was carrying a satchel of smoked fish, he accosted me in a much-too-familiar manner. I put him off and was surprised at how quickly he retreated into himself. There was no repeat of this incident — of which I was greatly heartened. Somehow I could not — after all I'd been through — be affectionate to this man.

On another occasion, maybe a month past our meeting of him, Will openly broached the subject of the captain helping us to escape. As the words left Will's eager mouth, I felt prickly all over. What if this man, whom we hardly knew, should now betray us?

The only others who knew of our plan were the fellow convicts whose lives depended upon our mercy. There were seven such men and they were tight-lipped, to say the least.

Captain Smith, who was seated on our only chair, stroked his chin at hearing Will's impromptu speech. His eyes turned to the harbor, and he regarded his ship.

Then he turned and faced each of us in turn. He shook his head. "Do you realize what you're asking me to do? The penalty would be death for all of us, myself included."

He let this sink in a good little while. Finally, his dark eyes sought mine, but I glanced away. Will was edgy and scratched his beard roughly. "Don't think we cannot pay," he said, his voice raised barely above a whisper.

At this, Captain Smith chuckled. He had a great round head on his shoulders, and a face that was either sullen or soft.

"Do you think I'd enjoy squeezing the thalers out of you good people? Is that what you think I am all about?" His brow was heavily creased. "Truth be known," he said as he puffed disgruntled on his pipe, "I loathe this English system all the way to its rotten core. The very idea!" He drew a great amount of smoke into him, and blew it away with a sigh.

As the smoke cleared, his face was different. He was chuckling again, his face red as an apple, and cheerful.

"I'll take you up on whatever you propose, Will Bryant — but not for money. I'll do it for the sand it'll put in the Crown's craw. Let them choke on that sand, I say." Then Captain Smith grew serious.

Will was relieved. Of a truth, we all breathed more easily,

now the cat was out of the bag. I was seated on the driftwood log I used at mealtimes, and the two children were at my feet — Charlotte playing a little hand-game with Emmanuel.

Shortly, I served the men native bread and steaming stew and there was good talk all around except that Will took too heartily to the captain's rum again. I warned him with my eyes against doing this, but his glance moved shiftily from mine.

Will was ever his own man, but there was a strange reck-lessness about him that night, which I didn't quite under-stand. There we were all set to free our family, and Will was running a-tick with his own wildness. He acted out his words too loudly, I thought; and his hands whirled about like the night bats that circled our hut.

A day or so later, two of Will's scruffy helpers showed up at our fire. They seemed to want something, so I gave them a cup of fish tea apiece, for which they grumbled apprecia-tion, and scrunched down on the sand. I must say, I liked neither of them.

The one was William Allen. He had a plain and old face. In any case, his cheeks were fallen in and he was sallow-faced and white-haired.

His mate, William Moreton, was a navigator — so he said. He claimed he was from somewhere south of Fowey. But I'd never laid eyes on him back home. He was lean and drawn, like everyone else. But there was a ratty look to his eye that made me uncomfortable. He barely spoke above a whisper. His eyes were thin as the wind and revealed nothing of his heart.

Together, both men gave me a little chill.

That night, Will said he had a bit of compromise to make.

"Is it about those two fellows of yours who came to sup with us?"

"Sorry, Mary."

I smelled the spirits on his breath. "What are you sorry for?"

"Those two. They've forced me to include them in our escape."

I felt my stomach tighten into a knot. I didn't know what to say. "That man Moreton called himself a navigator."

"He's had some experience, no doubt. But no way could I brush them off. They had me dead to rights — either we take them or they give us away."

I could barely believe this turn. "Are they at peace with us now?"

"They'll stay mum as long as we let them come."

"The more hands, the better," I said, trying to be hopeful. "Just don't talk about our plans with *anyone* else."

He rubbed his eyes. "Ah," he said, sighing. "I'm no better than a burden to you."

I let him think it, if he wanted to. And said no more. Better, I thought, that he should remember his deed than go forward and invent some new way to trip up our plans.

The Escape

Late March 1791

Our opportunity came sooner than we thought.

This was fortunate, because we only had until the end of March before the first gales started to blow, and would thus prevent us from traveling. So we knew the last chance to get off would be whenever the sea was flat and the sky was clear. This meant, too, waiting for the new moon, which was almost upon us.

All in one day, I got a chart, a compass, and a quadrant. While aboard the *Waaksamheyd,* delivering laundry, Captain Smith said to me, "Once you get free of this place, you must remember to follow the chart north, always north."

I told him we knew that full well. Our destination was Timor in the Dutch East Indies.

"Well, there's something else you probably know, but just in case you don't, I am going to mention it." His expression was darker than I'd ever seen it.

"What is it you wish to say?"

"That if Will doesn't lay off the rum, he's going to give your plans away. I heard him talking with some sailors here the other night, and he was pretty free with his tongue."

Captain Smith's lips tightened, and he shook his head.

"You must understand . . ." He paused, and his eyes swept the tall masts of his ship.

"I do, sir. You've put yourself quite on the line. We're in debt to you." I sought his eyes, but he looked around and around the ship, making sure that no one was listening to us. Finally, his eyes rested briefly on mine, and he returned, "That's the point." He sighed, rubbing his chin. "I'm so deep into this mess, I fear what could happen to me, not to mention my ship, and even my country. It's a treasonous act I'm engaged in, and whatever its merits, I've personal concerns — a wife and children."

"As do I, sir. But trust in Will, and I will watch him doubly and make sure he doesn't fly freely to the spirits."

He nodded formally, I thought, but then I saw that his first lieutenant was at hand, and he had very curious eyes for our conversation. Hastily, Captain Smith closed by saying, "There, young lady, that canvas bag of supplies should hold you."

"Thank you, Captain," I said, and stepped back, out of their way, and then disappeared over the rail and down the ladder to where Bennelong waited with our cutter.

It was true — what he said. Will was going afoul of us just then. In fact, I feared his drunken talk when he left me and crept off to the general camp. This he did each night. To put an honest face on the thing, I was more afraid of Will's loose tongue than I ever let on.

But how was I to stop him? What was I to do?

At that time, any infraction of Governor Phillip's law got a sentence of banishment into the desert. This was a fate worse than the executioner's rope. For if the beasts didn't get you, the sun surely would. None who were banished were heard from again. But their bones were always found, white as snow. Some fifty convicts fed the dingoes and crows. Their bleached remains left no doubt of what our fate — as exiles — would be, should we go into the desert.

Surprisingly, Will took this in stride. He laughed at any mention of our being found out and punished.

I spoke no more to Captain Smith about this, but kept it well to myself — only now I watched Will carefully.

Our plans were not attended by misfortune, however. Things moved swiftly on their course. We had a large cache under a platform inside our hut, in which we'd hidden our compass, quadrant, and chart. We also laid in one hundred pounds of flour and one hundred pounds of rice and fourteen pounds of salt pork. We stored away two old muskets and some rounds of ammunition. This was all to the good — as long as no one spoke of it. I was determined Will wouldn't, which meant making sure there was no rum around. To this end, Captain Smith did all his drinking alone and took no more meals with us.

Each day that passed, we grew more anxious to leave. With nine of us working, we filled the cache in two months' time. Nor was this all — Bennelong and Ngan helped us, too. Bennelong brought dried fruits and the sap of a tree that he explained was good for caulking the cutter. I collected sweet tea leaves that Ngan showed me how to pick, and these I wrapped in some ragged cloth.

When our time drew near, we put away all remorse and gladly thought only of freedom. Fortunately, Will and the rum flask did not meet up.

The dark moon night of our escape came at last. Putting the many hours of anticipation behind us, we were more than ready to run. That day the *Waaksamheyd* had set off for England; the *Supply* was gone to Norfolk Island. That left but one small boat — the cutter, the one we used for fishing — in the harbor.

This was the governor's own craft and he watched it closely — or had lookouts do so — most of the time. Therefore, we couldn't bring it in to shore at night, even on a dark night. However, when the time came and a cloudy night was upon us, Bennelong swam out alone. I wondered how he could dare to swim in that sharky water, but he did so willingly. Once out at the cutter's gunwale, he cut the hawser, and then towed her into shallow water. Thanks to God, we saw no fins.

As soon as this was done, we all waded in carrying supplies and, of course, the two children. The water was cold but calm.

We dared not hoist a sail, or row a stroke — the lookouts would have seen it. Instead, we let the cutter float out in the dark with the tide.

There we were, facing one another in the starlight — seven convicts and Will and me and the children, who were now three and a year and a half. Four of the escapees were men we knew and trusted: James Martin, Sam Bird, Nat Lilley, and James Cox.

William Moreton, William Allen, and Sam Broom were the newcomers, who'd sort of blackmailed their way in. I expected to keep a wary eye on them all the time, and I did from that night forward.

Thus we placed ourselves in God's care and watched the shore slip off and our little dark hut disappear in the darkness. Bennelong and Ngan waved once, then they, too, slipped away. I saw Bennelong once again, tall and clear against an outlying rock, before he fell back into the trees and was gone from sight.

Forthwith, we rounded the little island called Pinchgut, and past that we found the open sea, and were away.

We could contain ourselves no longer. Suddenly, the whole group of us — friends and strangers alike — began to shake hands and thump one another on the back. There we were beyond reach — for there was no craft to chase us down — and we had done it all in perfect secrecy.

Our plan worked as well as could be expected — if only the weather would hold out, and stay clear. I was, of course, fraught with worry for the children. But I was steadfast in my prayers and the knowledge that to stay at Botany Bay was certain death.

It was then I looked about me and saw the clear truth of it: I was the only woman. But of course I was a Cornwall girl. I knew the sea better than most and could read the sky better than some, and I could swim in the worst of weathers. Moreover, I had my wits about me — most of the time.

I glanced at Will at the tiller. He looked confident, strong. I wished Captain Smith could see him now — could see all of us, in fact. But he was long gone on his own sea voyage, and so we turned to ours.

The
Sea
Run

For all of that night and the next day, we sailed north within hazy sight of the land. The chart showed that we must ride the bad weather along the deserted coast for some thousand miles or more. This thought stuck in my mind.

Was it possible to go so far in an open boat? Rumors from Captain Smith told us of someone who'd sailed that far. His name was Bligh.

Verily, it seemed impossible. Yet that was what we had to do, or die trying. I vowed we'd do it. But as I looked into the faces of the others, I wondered who would make it, and who wouldn't.

Sam Broom, the largest of the newcomers, had the look of someone tough and durable. Sad-eyed Moreton had brought him, saying he was an old friend.

James Martin, as I've said before, was a better companion than any, and he and little Nat Lilley were really trustworthy — I had no doubt of that. Neither one was youthful, but they were steadfast and sure, and they never complained. James was a bright spark in the darkest of times.

In the following days, my uneasiness about sallow old Allen and pale, shifty Moreton changed somewhat, as they proved themselves most melancholic and quiet, but hard to the oar. I liked them the better for that, I can tell you.

Sam Bird, whom I've hardly mentioned, was true to his name — small and flighty of movement. He was always making excuses for himself, apologizing for nothing — if he bumped someone, or if he drank too much water.

For better or worse, these men were the sailors of our ship and we were as bonded to them as they were latched to us, heart and soul — or so we then believed.

For two days we kept on northward, driven by a steady northeast wind. Midway into the second day, an argument started between Will and Sam Broom over some matter of navigation. Will shouted him down, but there was bad blood between them now.

Sam, as I've said, was a big man. Square of jaw, large of frame. Much larger than Will. This little war that had brewed up between them was risky, to say the least. In such close quarters, we had to be so very careful of our moods and our actions.

How could you be mad at someone you couldn't see past, or get around, and who was always there like the sky or the sea?

The cutter itself was but twenty-two feet long with a

beam of six feet, and eleven of us were thrown in the middle of it. In rough seas, which was how they were, it was hard enough to just stay afloat, let alone worry about how you were getting along with the man at your elbow.

Of a truth, the wind and water was always up, and the cutter was in constant danger of swamping. And this odd crew was bailing most of the time — and everyone took their turn at this, even little Charlotte, who thought of it as fun.

On the third morning, the wind died.

We spied an inlet and some dry ground not far off the star-board bow. Our water supply was in a ten-gallon barrel — if we were to survive, this had to be kept full. Anyway, in toward shore we went, nip and tuck all the way. Choppy waves sluiced over the cutter and drenched us to the bone.

At last we caught the land breeze just right, and sped for-ward at even keel into a river's mouth. This estuary was bor-dered by low hills and mangrove trees. We rounded-to in the lee of a long, wooded point and oared hard until the keel ground on the sand.

Will hopped out and shouted, "I'm calling this place For-tunate Cove."

We all got out then and felt the firm footing of the coast. It felt very good to be on dry land again, and not bobbing all about. Soon a party of friendly natives showed up. They were curious and offered us no harm. We gave them some clothes; they were much satisfied.

One tall, dark man covered with a fine, white filigree of tattoos gave us a gift of grouper, a huge fish. We thanked him, and then set off — Will and I — to find the hearts of palm that Bennelong had taught us to harvest. Once cooked, this food tasted much like cabbage. It proved a warm belly-ful along with the grouper that I baked in the hot ash. The meal, served just around sundown, was most wonderful.

Thus we ate happily with our fingers while listening to the odd squeaks and shrieks of the night settling birds.

After our meal, the men drifted off down along the wa-terway. Some while later, James Martin reappeared, grinning, with a round black thing in his hands. Studying it, I discov-ered immediately that it was a solid rock of black coal.

"Found it on the beach, Mary," he said, beaming. We fin-gered the coal in wonder — as did the children, who found its dark, sea-polished gleam something amazing.

"This was just laying in the sand?" I asked.

"Yes," said he, all smiles. "And where there's one, there's got to be more."

"Wouldn't it be good," said William Moreton, his face an-imated for the first time since I'd met him, "if we found a whole mine of it?"

Scoffed William Allen, "And what would we do with it, then? Open up a store?"

Moreton shrugged and looked shifty-eyed from face to face.

But the one who was charmed with the idea was Sam Bird. He danced about the fire like a daft little gnome, chuckling gleefully. "Coal, coal," he sang.

And the children clapped to the beat of his bare feet.

Well, as fate would have it, some more of the stuff was found — within moments, too. On the campfire the coal lumps hissed. They glowed steadfast as the night crept around and the stars came out.

Full-bellied, Charlotte lay on my lap and slept contentedly. Emmanuel was still at the breast, sleeping and suckling.

The first stars glimmered. We lay out, the lot of us, sprawled on the sand near our cheerful coal-fire, which reminded us of home. I gave thanks for getting this far.

From that time forward, bad things beset us on a regular basis. Our boat began to leak, making it necessary to put into shore every few days to caulk it. This we accomplished with the beeswax and rosin that Bennelong had given us. Yet it worked only for a short time and there was such a small supply that we worried greatly.

We had another problem as well. All of us were badly

smitten by the sun. Of course, we hadn't any hats or other protection but to tie a wad of shirt about the head. Little Charlotte got burned all on her arms and cheeks, and she cried whenever touched. I covered Emmanuel in an ancient shawl, and he was the better of the two.

The men's faces, bearded and dark, were somewhat protected, but their lips split and caused them great pain.

Days passed without event, though, while we endured these woes. Fortunately, the wind was strong in our sail and the Great Barrier Reef was now to the lee of us. The glittering sea made a soft roar as it washed over the coral.

"Now, *that* is a sight," I exclaimed when we first came upon it. The white reef clawed by the surf seemed to stretch forever.

"Four hundred miles we've come, Mary," said Will proudly.

In the grand scheme of things, it was but a little way. Actually, the end of the reef — and far beyond that — was our goal. The distant island we sought was called Timor. Best not to think of that, for closer by was a string of islands all along the main portion of New South Wales and New Holland. These would make good harbor and safe mooring — if we could get to them.

After seven more days at sea, while creeping along the outside of the reef, we found a way through the coral to the other side. Beyond this was a small, palm-fringed island set in a sky-blue bay. Our need to put ashore was pressing. We hadn't been on land in some time because whenever we found a likely place, there were hostile natives waiting for us on the beach.

Many times we were driven back to sea by sharp-pointed spears.

Yet this little island seemed so remote and the beach on the farther shore was absent of men. So we put in without much difficulty and started to gather some food, wood, and water. Will went into the palms but returned immediately. He had his shirt off, and he was carrying it like a satchel. Something was inside it.

"Look, Mary," he called out. His eyes glittered as he laid the shirt open on the sand.

"Turtle eggs."

"The best you've ever seen — and none rotten."

"I'll have a taste of one of those," said a rough voice.

Sam Broom swooped out a hand and crushed one of the eggs into his open mouth. The yolk ran down his chin.

"There'll be none of that," snapped Will.

Broom wiped his mouth with the back of his hand. "I do as I please," he said.

"You'll do as we say," James Martin said. He was folding a net very near to where Broom was standing.

Broom, who was now joined by Moreton and Allen, growled an oath and stomped off. We could see from his heaving shoulders how angry he was. The three of them went off a-grumbling.

"That's a man with a grudge against God," James said after Broom and his friends had gone away into the sea grapes.

Sooner or later, some blows would come of this. But I couldn't think about that now — there was food to prepare. Will, James, and Nat found palm hearts and more turtle eggs.

Sam Broom, for all his roughness, brought back a big sea turtle. He, Moreton, and Allen butchered it, letting no one else lend a hand. But then they shared the meat with the rest of us quite gladly. They seemed to relish the fact of finding something bigger and more important than Will's little eggs. That and their skill at butchering made all three tolerable and friendly that night.

However, they later took to drink — the three and Will. And while they celebrated their good feelings in the firelight — and the spell of enmity was off of them for the time being — I looked on with pity. For I knew that friendship built on the enchantment of rum ends badly.

Soon after we left the island, the summer monsoons struck. The weather got foul. I began to share the tiller with none other than Moreton, who turned out to be a good navigator, just as he'd said. Tiller in hand, he plowed us through the brine with a small, thin smile printed on his lips. He took sleepless turns with James Cox and with me. I hadn't expected Moreton to turn out to be what he'd said.

Will and Moreton both used the quadrant, the compass, and the chart, arguing sometimes over means and measures. But they always came back on the right tack. We did all right, too, except for the awful buffeting we took. Not to mention the sleepless nights, the leg cramps, and the seasickness. We got cross and quarrelsome, but stifled our grievances as soon as we came into the big swells that nearly overturned our boat. Mostly, Charlotte and Emmanuel were quiet. Weak from lack of food and water, they spent much of the time sleeping.

The sky lay like lead overhead, spitting rain. Now the cutter took on more water than we were able to bail. So we threw off some of our things — food and water stayed, but everything else went. Bundled clothing and some tools, mostly, went into the green and angry sea.

We bailed day and night and slept sitting up, holding on to the thwarts, and chattering with cold. The men were so dispirited, so hangdog. I began to think they were giving up without a fight.

Then Sam Bird flapped his arms and crowed out, "By God, we're trumped, we're leveled, we're doomed." He said this, sang this, while I stared into his sea-crazed eyes and told him, "You've no call to quit now, Sam Bird. We've hardly started."

James Martin, the rain running off his chin, hollered his own chant into the wind. "Never," he cried. "Never." He said it with such a good, gut-wrenching yell that he awakened William Allen, whose knuckles were fairly scraping the gunnels. Allen was sickish, but he rallied. James prodded the lot of seasick ones into action — "Hove to, heave to, hove to" — and he battled with the oar drill, making the men behave.

I tossed my own gall into the brew — giving everyone a piece of my mind while I held on to Emmanuel for dear life, and kept my other arm around Charlotte.

Moreton held to the tiller, a grim thrust to his chin and a gritty cast to his eye. That night, I surely banished any thought I had previous of his character. He was the sad-eyed captain of chaos, riding us up to the top of one comber and down into the trough of another — with nary a flaw in his delivery of up-and-over.

But aside from him and James Martin and my Will, the rest of the sea dogs had their tails between their legs.

I gave them a good bit of hiding, I must say — and, coming from a woman, it worked.

"Giving up, boys?" I said — for they were all white and weak and holding on when they should've been pounding oars.

"Why, I've never seen such cowardliness. My own children outshine the likes of you. Look at yourselves. You're not dogs; I take that back — you're lambs, fresh for the slaughter."

And I *baaed* at them to make them feel even worse — and the effect it had, well, I hardly know how to put it. They jumped.

Sam Broom, who was one of the worst laggards, came around quick — "Do what she says," he threatened.

And, for the first time since the storm fell upon us, he acted like the big man he was and put his muscle hard to the oar.

"Now, all of you!" I shouted over the sea wrath.

And Nat Lilley and James Cox let go of the thwarts and began battering the brine with their oars, too.

Up we went to the top of a soaring emerald slope, and the cutter was a plaything amidst the gales. We were knocked about so badly that our bones rang with the jarring and jolting of the oarlocks and the pummeling of the sea.

Yet the men kept quiet after I lay into them; they kept to the task.

Early toward morning, Moreton fell exhausted from the tiller, and I took his station while Will steadied my hand and held the children, too. Nor was this all — the sun never shone that day, nor for eight days after.

And we saw no sight of land under the heavy canopy of leaden cloud. Always, the towering top-heavy swells threatened to drown us, and the storm continued to play with our craft as if it were a great, cruel cat and we were but a wee, small sea mouse.

The food that we had was hard grains of uncooked rice and some jerked crayfish. The barrel of water we dared not touch in the badness of weather, for fear it would spill.

At the end of these eight dreadful days, and the lashing of the sea still at our backs, we were blown, half-dead, to a small deserted island.

Up we crunched onto the gloamy sand — and, just like that, the bad weather let up, and like an answered prayer, the evening sun showed his full face and put a crimson light upon the world. After that, the clouds thinned to horsetails and the wind came up and whistled it all away. A gentle rain in the fading sunlight brought forth a double rainbow. As we admired it, one foot of the rainbow touched down on the sand where we lay — exhausted and half-drowned — but yet alive.

Our island, within the Great Barrier Reef, was wreathed in birds. Their high, thin, piercing cries were music to our ears. For the first time, the boom of the breakers lay away from us, striking the reef some hundred yards off. All that first night on the low, anvil-shaped island, it rained on and off, and we were thus able to capture freshwater to drink.

In the morning, when a crowd of bilious yellow clouds started to break, Nat Lilley went off a ways and found some turtles that had come ashore to lay their eggs. We all brought two of them back to our camp, and Sam Broom butchered and smoked the meat. Whilst this went on, I collected as much wild cabbage as I could haul back to camp.

In so doing I discovered a rookery on the white sand. The sad, poor birds were quite unwilling to leave their nests, for it was laying season. All I had to do was take them up with my hands — they weren't affrighted of me at all, which made it all the worse. But now we had an abundance of meat and eggs and water, and things were looking up for us — or so we thought.

On the fifth night of our stay, some strange canoes cut through the horns of the reef, and came most spiritedly our way. These were natives of a different kind from the ones we'd gotten used to. For one thing, they had high-prowed canoes with sails made of wooden reeds and they flew through the foaming sea.

"Put out the fire," I told Sam. "There's danger coming."

Then, gathering the children up, I got them to shelter — a little cave set behind the sea grapes. If no one peeked in, it was shelter enough to hide the lot of us — all crouching and wondering what would happen next.

"What are they doing?" Will whispered to me, as I was closest to the cave mouth and had a good eye on what stirred.

"They're all about fixing their suppers," I returned.

"How many?" asked Sam Broom.

"Thirty . . . or more."

Then I told them more of what I could see — one old crone was cooking fish over coals. The men carried big clamshells out of their canoes, and the shells were smoking. Soon, I understood that these were full of hot fire-coals. Thus these people traveled about with fire, and could cook wherever they went. And they were doing so now — some laughing and talking whilst others were spear-fishing. But no one made any effort to explore or seek out the place where we were hidden. It was a good thing Nat Lilley and James Martin and Will had brushed away our tracks in the sand. After eating, the natives sang songs, after which, without further ado, they all went to sleep.

We stayed holed up in our cave, quiet as mice. It was hot, and the mosquitoes pecked at us most persistently. But as we didn't raise a sound, we were safe. Before first light, the natives pushed off in their canoes, and soon they were gone from sight.

After coming out of hiding, we prepared some rice and shellfish in the following manner: We got a little fire going and we put sea rocks into it. When the rocks were hot enough we dropped them into a tiny tide pool. Into this we poured our rice and rock lobsters and other mollusks. This was the best food we'd had.

Before we left the island that morning, we found a tree with fruit on it that looked like bell pepper, however, the taste was more satisfactory. We ate these heartily. James Martin and William Moreton then put turtle fat on the underside of the cutter. This, they said, would fix the leaks. Stormy weather was now upon us, and the day opened dark and dour.

Mid-May 1791

Ten days went by after we left the island, during which we saw no others. The sky darkened down, and held us cheerless and withdrawn. The sea spanked us at all turns of the sail.

We came then upon a kind of immense lagoon in which the shadowy shapes of gray, cow-faced dugongs swam. They nosed the boat freely, showing no fear at all.

"Why, they're just big, fat mermaids!" said Sam Bird, all crinkle-eyed, laughing.

"What must they think of our condition?" William Allen asked, scratching his white beard.

"You think they've ever seen good old St. Nicholas in the flesh?" James Martin joked.

"I am red and white," chuckled William Allen, whose sunburn and beard fit the bill.

Everyone laughed a little at this — the first time any of us had heard laughter in quite some time.

And while we rowed, the gray beasts breathed mist all around us, and followed us until we lost them later that afternoon.

After another couple of days, we saw a barren patch of sand and headed right for it. There was no cover on this whale-shaped strait. But there were dugong bones piled up into columns of phantoms.

Who did this? What did it mean?

We stopped on the strait and rested for a spell, while all of us had a good look at the great piles of dugong rib bones. Charlotte took a special interest in the way they were piled. She wanted very much to climb upon them — yet I felt uneasy and wouldn't let her. It was as if some unseen presence was watching us the whole time we were there.

At the apex of each pile there was a bleached white turtle shell — put there for such effect as to appear like a kind of towering head. Under the bluish shadows of the bone towers, we made sweet tea. As we drank from cups that James Cox had carved from cedar burls, a strange sense of communion came over us. It was as if we were in some kind of ancient church of the open sky. Maybe it was the sight of all the bleachy bones, I don't know, but for no reason in particular I asked Sam Broom to tell me what his crime was, how he'd gotten himself here, of all places. . . .

After Sam Broom said, "Stole three small pigs," each man in our midst said his own crime.

Sam Bird: "I stole bread."

James Cox: "I took cherry wood for a cabinet."

James Martin: "I stole old lead and iron."

William Allen: "I took twenty-nine handkerchiefs."

Nat Lilley: "I took a fishnet, a watch, and two spoons."

William Moreton: "So help me God, I don't remember what I took."

Will Bryant: "I smuggled cargo and I assaulted a revenue officer."

I was last, and I finished it off with: "I stole a silk bonnet."

It was curious the way the men smiled at this sudden confession of mine and how they lingered in silence, sipping their tea and thinking.

Afterward, we wandered among the bones, feeling, I believe, a closer kindred spirit than before. For it was, in truth, the petty things we did that got us to that spit of sand where we were each needful of the other. Our crimes, once confessed, seemed so much the same — so little and so dreary.

The following day, the sun came out with a vengeance. The water burned. I couldn't shake my thoughts of the men and their confessions. I kept hearing their voices tolling their petty crimes. As I worked the tiller to the lee of the reef, I considered how some of these men were too old now to make a new life. They looked and acted too woebegone and given-up-on-themselves. The youngest, of course, were Will and me. The oldest was William Allen, who was somewhere around fifty-five.

Mostly they were in their forties or fifties — and they really showed it, with gap-toothed sunken faces and bony bodies reddened in the fierce, unstoppable sun. They were, all in all, a very sad lot — yet their hearts were good, and there wasn't one among them who didn't pick a pretty flower for Charlotte, or hold Emmanuel while I cooked.

That night, though, without any warning, a fight broke out. We were momentarily becalmed when it happened.

Will said, "Pull that oar, you lout!" Sam was staring out to sea, with a wicked look in his eye. He got that way, sometimes. Dark and strange as the Devil.

"I'll pull when I'm good and ready," Sam said.

"That's enough, you two," I cried. Yet, if they heard me, they acknowledged me not one whit, and then Will charged forward, tripping over William Moreton. He grabbed at Sam Broom's beard, caught it, and jerked his head to where he could also take ahold of his ear.

The two wrestled, most furious and savage, among the brine and parrot fish we'd netted that morning. One was up and the other down. They rolled round, snorting like beasts.

James Martin, hot Irish that he was, took sides at once. He was our man, and he held back Sam's huge fists.

Nonetheless, Will got head-knocked some hard blows. He gave his own as well, but there was no tallying this sort of thing, as the boat rocked precariously and just about cap-sized entirely. At the same time, a nosy shark closed in and bumped the tiller and broke my clasp on it.

The huge fish was grayish and white-faced. Bigger than any shark had a right to be. He was almost as long as the cut-ter and about as thick. Now, with the two men fighting and rocking the boat, we found ourselves in real danger.

I screamed in Will's ear, "Let go, you're going to capsize the boat!" Again, the shark bumped the wood under my hand.

"He wants the bloody tiller," I said, and Will pressed up close to my shoulder and then shoved me back, the blood dripping from his nose.

"That blood'll do us worse injury with the shark," James Martin said as he wiped Will's face with his own shirtsleeve.

Meanwhile, the shark took hold of the tiller and gave it a good pull.

"If he gets ahold of that, we're lost," said Nat Lilley.

"I can make another one," James Cox added. "All I need's my whittlin' knife and a piece of driftwood."

"Sit down — all of you," I ordered.

By now both of my children were crying. Charlotte had started doing so when the fight broke out, and now she was wailing to split our ears. Emmanuel was taking in great gulps of air and sobbing.

The cutter then received a severe bump at the keel; we wobbled precariously. If half the men hadn't righted her, she'd have gone over. But she didn't; she flopped back and rocked side to side. The big shark came nosing at us from all directions.

"He smells the bloody turtle fat we used for caulking," said Will.

Will was right. Then he put in, "If he wants some turtle flesh so bad, we'll give it him!" William Allen uncapped our food barrel and brought out the smoked turtle meat.

The cat-eyed shark was at the tiller again. But his mouth wasn't lined up proper with that idiot's half-smile of his, all wide open, and he couldn't do it — as I was flashing the tiller before his face.

We were then very near a big sea rock coming off the reef. By pulling toward it, we might find a fast and quick mooring — plus it was tall enough to accommodate the lot of us and keep us well out of harm's way. So we moored and climbed onto this black promontory.

At the same time, Nat Lilley threw another hunk of turtle meat to the lee of the shark. He went for it, straight and clean, and that gave us all the time we needed to get up well away from him.

The way that shark tore into the meat told me how lucky we were. No one wanted to go back to the boat for a good while. We perched on the rock and waited until the shark was gone about his business before we resumed our sea voyage.

A close call.

As we dried out, so to put it, we looked into the clear sea and saw all manner of creatures there. Not only fish but long, kelpie-looking sea snakes that hung in the current with their flat, bright-marked sides shining in the salt water. More turtles — but we didn't chase after them.

Later in the day we resolved to go, and shoved off. The two fighters, Will and Sam, were contrite as ever could be.

As we sailed northward toward the Straits of Endeavor, the rainy weather that had attended us for so long quit. The sun beat down on us with painful ferocity. At this stage of our journey the long line of reef that we had had on our right hand for so many hundreds of miles now began to run closer to the mainland.

We passed through vast numbers of small islands, most of them very low and sandy and covered with bush. Others were of greater size and had high trees on them. Although the wind blew very strong from the south and east, the sea was smooth, and the Great Reef proved an excellent barrier against the violence of the waves.

We seldom ventured to the mainland now because the natives were still so numerous and so hostile. At night we saw their fires flickering on the beaches. They used the islands for their fishing camps, and we had to be extra careful.

Our occasional forays to find freshwater proved quite dangerous — often one of us would be chased at spearpoint, or a hail of arrows would come raining out of the shadows of trees. No one was seriously hurt, but Sam Bird got sea urchin needles in his feet, and so did some of the others when they came dashing back to the boat, chased by a crowd of fierce-painted men.

Other woes persisted, too. The mosquitoes kept us awake at all hours, with their whining and bloodletting. Some of the trees leaked poison from the leaves, and all of us, at one time or another, got burned by these poison-trees.

Will and I seemed to be at bad ends, too — arguing and feuding over things of ill importance. The children, weakened and sickened, cried from want of food. Our stores were all gone except for a little hard rice. In this condition, we spent more time foraging during the day as our boat went along its way. The fish of the reef were still plentiful, and Will's good luck and skill with the net was one of the things that providence had blessed us with.

Yet we were tired and fought amongst ourselves. Hunger and lack of comfort had hardened our hearts and made us crazy.

One night, while we were staying on a miserable small islet where the sting of the mosquitoes was most painful, Will disappeared. No one seemed to have seen him leave, but at dusk, as we prepared our supper of parrot fish and grunt and hind, I went to look for Will among the twisted trees.

I found him sitting on a little hillock overlooking the bay, head in hands.

I was struck by what I heard more than by what I saw, for I'd seen him in despair many times before. But here he was — crying like Emmanuel. The tears coursing down his bearded cheeks, and him unreasoning in his outburst, saying that God was to blame for our bad condition.

I was frightened by this, alarmed and put off — a grown man in such a broken state — and I hung back, momentarily, trying to think what next to do.

"Will," said I, after a moment's wait, "the Bible says desire is the root of all evil, and poverty the worst of all snares. Do you not see that it's the Devil himself who's brought you to this?"

Startled, he stared into my eyes. "We'll not see many morrows, Mary," he answered.

The hope — I readily saw — was all gone out of him. But not, I daresay, out of me. As it says in the Bible, "Help the weak if you are strong." I felt the strength rise within me then, and I told Will that we'd live to enjoy all the sunrises God made for us to see — no fewer and no more.

"Despair," I continued, "is the Devil's handmaiden."

"She is at my side all the while — and him breathing in my ear."

"That's mosquitoes, not the Devil."

I took his head in my hands and he wept all the more as I did so. I cradled him as if he were a babe. Right quick, he quieted. My fear, just then, was that one of our party would see him thus, and report it to the rest. They were all a bit like Will, coming undone and acting mutinous strange, but he was by far the worst.

"Get up now, Will," I told him.

His hands were all a-tremble, his face drained and tired. He obeyed in silence. We walked back across the spur of sand and through the thickets to our camp.

The next day, while continuing our journey north and west, Nat Lilley, who so far had proved an exemplary fellow, suddenly went all crazy, saying he saw the streets of London loom before him.

He jumped out of the boat and swam foolishly for shore. I was a great way toward the back of the cutter, so could do nothing one way or the other. Surprisingly, no one made a move to stop Nat or to help him. Out of empty eyes, we sat and stared.

Nat was no swimmer — not before, not now. He floundered helpless, and I saw him swallow some seawater.

"Won't someone get in there and save this man?" I asked in a pitch of anger.

No one moved or lifted a hand, or even turned to face me. They kept their eyes fixed on Nat, who was now going under for the last time. It was then I jabbed Will with my fist and ordered him to do something fast, and, thanks to God, he did. He took up his fishnet and cast it bravely and neatly over Nat, in such a way as to drag him in. At the same time, as we'd gone off course and drifted toward land, a crowd of natives, all of them armed with spears, came out to meet us.

It seemed we'd be killed on the spot — for these hostile tribesmen were close enough to swim to us — and yet frantic and nearly drowning Nat was still not in the boat. I enjoined Will to hurry it up. Then I stood up and, knowing not what else to do, I sang a nursery song. It went like this:

"Sing, sing,
What shall I sing?
The cat's run away
With the pudding string!
Do, do,
What shall I do?
The cat's run away
With the pudding too!"

The men on the beach listened. I sang the same refrain several times more as Will hauled Nat in. I shall never forget the faces of those natives — they looked upon me most strangely, yet the anger had fled from them, and all that was left was a kind of mute wonder.

✹   ✹   ✹

We had time to correct our course and to guide the cutter reefward, away from danger. When at last I sat down, I was all a-shiver. The song was over, but I still had the shakes from singing it.

"There, there, Mary," Will said. He put his hand on my shoulder, and at the same time, Charlotte hugged me.

Nat babbled. Sunstruck he was, his head ringing with unreason. James Martin gave me a glad hand and a fine smile.

"You saved the day again, Mary," he said softly.

I saw the others nod at this, and a few grumbled out more praises and thanks, but I slunk to the ribs of the boat and hid my face in the arms of my children. Never had I been so sure of sudden defeat at the hands of foes, and yet never had I been so thankful of deliverance moments after. For the rest of that day we continued our course close to the Great Reef, and saw nothing more of hostiles.

The days passed unevenly, with equal amounts of good and bad weather, and the usual hardship of not enough food and no place to get freshwater.

When we looked at the chart, we realized we were now in the Gulf of Carpentaria. A peninsula lay to the west of this gulf — that thought was comforting — but once past it, the great open water stretched all the way to Timor, some hundreds of miles away.

Will was quite good with the sextant. Surprisingly, I'd gotten on with the tiller and did most of the steering. We feared to lay up on land, as there were now tribesmen watching us from the shore.

Our water barrel was nearly dry. At night we were forced to land on bare-boned islets and to lap rainwater off the clefts of rocks like dogs. One night we passed an island that tempted us with the thought of game. We pulled ashore, and James Cox chased a big, ungodly bird, but it got away in the dark. The thing ran on two legs like a man, but was covered in a fur of feathers.

This shore was muddy and densely thicketed with mangrove roots, in which there were hidden crocodiles and hanging serpents.

Sam Broom loaded both muskets and, being the best shot, carried one of them with him. William Allen carried the other weapon, and the others bore fishing spears in the hope of sighting a wild pig. Will carried our bailing buckets with James Martin.

I stayed in the cutter, which was moored a little ways out, with the children, who were now sick with fever. I asked Nat Lilley, who had recovered from his sun-madness, to fetch me some sweet tea leaves, if he saw any. He promised to do so.

Whilst the men went a-hunting, I saw a large sea turtle close by the boat. Netting it without much hardship, I then discovered I wasn't strong enough to draw it aboard. So I made fast with it to an oarlock. The struggle with the turtle left me panting and gasping. I was much weakened from lack of food.

Time passed. I listened to the drone of insects and the cries of seabirds. Then Will and James appeared out of the mangroves. Their buckets were full.

"We found a fresh pool of springwater, Mary," Will said.

I took the buckets, one at a time, and poured them into our barrel. Several times they returned with more, and soon the barrel was half-full.

Once, James came up, all out of breath. "Stepped on a croc," he said.

Said Will, "I saw it slide you almost off your feet."

"Look," I said. "I caught a turtle."

Suddenly, all the men came a-running.

Behind them — a mob of natives.

Everyone splashed into the little bay.

A spear struck the side of the cutter and glanced off as I pushed the children down with my hand and peered over the side.

Hastily clawing, the men came onto the cutter and hunkered to their oars. Sam raised his musket and fired. A bolt of lightning spat out of the gun. The noise that followed was deafening. As the natives scattered, Sam dropped his weapon, lifted anchor, and we rowed off as fast as possible. William Allen left them with a parting shot from his gun. Yet, within minutes, two war canoes appeared out of the bush. This party of hostiles wasn't going to give up.

They'd have caught us, too, but we set a lucky sail and, just in time, the breeze billowed it out full and we got away.

Still, the war canoes followed us for some time, hanging back ever farther on the night sea as we tacked and held the wind, and fled to the north.

That last was our final good-bye to land. What was left of our voyage was the sea — no more landfalls and only the open water, as I was saying before. No turning back. What remained in our barrel was all the water we owned. But it was enough if we rationed it well and we had some rain.

The turtle I'd caught furnished us with blood to drink. Its sweetmeats we ate raw. Its flesh, too. This creature saved our lives. After it was gone, we had some rain. Our mouths open to the sky, we swallowed thankfully whilst our barrel did the same.

After that, the weather was clear and windy. For the following two weeks we braved the open sea and staved off thoughts of the most fearful kind. It rained ofttimes in the night, and we caught more drops on our tongues.

One night I awoke with a start. It seemed the heavens had dropped into the ocean. All around the cutter there were glowing bits of fallen stars, greenish and beautiful, and seemingly alive. No one else saw this miracle — just me. I believed it was a sign telling me that we would live to see the sight of land.

Moreover, after the starfall, we had cloudy weather that eased our sunburned skin. Some more days passed. Then James Martin glimpsed something. "Mary," he cried out. "There's some blue behind those clouds."

"The sky," said listless Nat Lilley.

Yet William Moreton saw it, too. "A darker blue than the sky," he exclaimed.

Then we saw — or thought we saw — a darkish thing on the horizon. So it went all that day, but a little before sunset, we doubted it no longer. To the north we saw what appeared to be a group of small islands. Then at nightfall these came together. The image of them held fast before the eye. They were, it seemed, not little pieces of disjointed land, but one great piece of magnificent earth. And it never moved, but remained still like a giant becalmed whale.

Timor

June 1791

We reached Koupang on the island of Timor the afternoon of the following day. A great assemblage of people
gathered to see us at harborside. No doubt, we were a de-
plorable looking lot: Our skins burned, our lips cracked, our
clothes hanging off our backs. The children were suffering
worse than any of us. Fever and chills and fits of dizziness.
Also, half-starved and delirious.

However, once we landed, the Dutch showed us their
utmost kindness. The governor of the island was present
and he interviewed Will straightaway. But, sad to say, Will
was too sick to speak with him. James Martin, with his quick
tongue, took over, and sort of saved the day, for the governor was bent on knowing who we were and where we'd
come from.

"I am Timotheus Wanjon," said the governor from under
his flat-brimmed straw hat. He was pale as a whitefish and
dressed in formal, ambassadorial clothing. We felt naked in
his presence.

"And I — am James Martin, your honor." And he gave a
little tremulous bow and polite wave of the hand.

"Ah, you're English then," the governor said, surprised.
"From the looks of you, I thought you'd be natives of

some kind." His long and drawn face cracked into a wide smile.

James knew the drill by heart, as did the rest of us, for we'd discussed it at length during the days at sea. Anyway, he lost no time in telling Governor Wanjon what had befallen us on the main.

"Some ten weeks ago," he began, "this bedraggled crew you see before you was nicely secured aboard the English commercial vessel, *Titan*."

"Where were you headed, sir?"

"To Port Jackson. But we got cracked up badly in a storm somewhere off the Gulf of Carpentaria. This is all that's left, I'm afraid."

The governor glanced at us, and shook his head. "You don't say . . . but how many lost?"

James made as if counting. His green eyes grew thoughtful with reminiscence. "All in all, I have it at one hundred seventeen, sir."

The Timorians believed it — wholeheartedly — as did their kind and worthy governor, who felt so sorry for us that he quickly arranged for our sorry contingent to rest up in some cottages that were usually reserved for visitors of state. We then proceeded from the dockyards to the gentle green interior of the island by carriage. We seemed almost to float up the spacious promenade made of crushed shell.

How wholesome and fine was the solid earth under our sea-spent feet when at last we arrived in front of the two cottages that the governor requisitioned for our use. Forthwith, we were given plentiful food and drink, and medical attention was offered to all who needed it, but especially to Will and the children, who had already collapsed in bed.

In addition, an Indian woman was stationed there with us to attend upon my family day and night.

Nor was this all — when we were settled in, some Dutch soldiers brought us new clothing, the smell of which brought tears to my eyes. I breathed it in, the scent of clean woven cotton. I wept in gratitude for the kindness of these people — who knew us not at all. Had they known, of course, our reception would've been quite different. I shuddered to think of that.

After some little rest on a real bed, which had the softness of a cloud, I checked on Will and the children. They were deep asleep, and peacefully so.

I walked out onto the veranda. The hour was that time of gold just before sunset. All the leaves were bathed in amber light. I watched a hummingbird dart about the flower beds. It seemed my soul had fallen into the body of a total stranger, someone who was living another life.

And then the Indian woman, whose name was Avaiyar, called to me. She'd prepared a table of delicacies among which I found chicken, roasted chicken! This I hadn't tasted since I'd left Cornwall. I wanted, more than anything, to share this repast. To eat with Will and the children, but Avaiyar thought they were too ill to eat, and so there I was — trembling with hunger and the steam from that roasted chicken rising up into the still air.

I sat and ate until my belly hurt. With every bite I thanked the Lord for bringing me to this table, for making me strong enough to care for the rest. So I ate not only for my sake but also for my family's.

Two days of idyllic rest passed by. During which time Will grew better, as did Charlotte. But Emmanuel remained feverish and bedridden, and there was little we could do for him except pray for his immediate recovery.

Within the week James Martin of the silver tongue began to tell our tale to anyone who would listen. The newspaper called me "The girl from the sea who saved so many . . ." and this wearisome thing got passed around so often that I tired of hearing it, but yet there was no stopping it. Nor was this all — this lie was a trifle compared to what was added on. Heaps of boasting about my bravery and heroism.

Such frivolity left little impression on me, however; I humored it. Unfortunately, Will didn't. He took any comment of me so badly that I found myself always worried about his disposition. He was given some drams of medicine for his ague, but his hands shook when he took it. Will's jealousy made him a dark figure to contend with — for any and all.

I said to him one afternoon that first week, "Will, won't you let go of yourself and just enjoy this bountiful heaven we have here?"

He lay upon his pillow on the floor, his face damp with sweat, his eyes glazed and fixed on me. "I leave the fun part of this affair to you, Mary," he answered dryly.

Said I, "Will, we've come so far! Can't you appreciate our success?"

"We're prisoners," he replied.

"How so?"

He waved his right hand at the tall, stately glass windows. "Think you this is heaven?" he asked pointedly.

"If we make it so."

"This is . . . ah . . . transportation," he groaned.

I said nothing.

"Mary, it's a pretty prison we have here. Sooner or later, we'll wind up in another dungeon, mark my words."

I wondered — was it just the sickness speaking?

Or was it the truth?

I looked at him and saw that he meant every word of it. A chill, as of the cold Cornish north wind, came into my bones, unbidden.

"Do you trust no one then?" I asked.

He propped himself up on his elbow. Staring at the tin-roofed ceiling, he laughed halfheartedly. "Don't worry, Mary, I won't ruin your show."

Our conversation was interrupted then by a soldier, who said, "I present his honor, the governor."

In he came, too, all of a sudden. Cheerful as the breeze, and straightaway — much to my disappointment because of Will — he shook out the latest newspaper story of my courage at sea.

"I give you the highest degree of honor," he swore. Then, looking over at Will, he added, "You, too, my man."

"You must know," said the tall Dutchman, flicking a little beetle off his dark suit of clothes, "that your renowned Captain Bligh sailed his boatload of survivors to Timor, just as you've done."

He gave me a pleasant little wink, and continued.

"I daresay, you know the story of your countryman. Why, it's almost two years since he left and went back to England."

Governor Wanjon smiled and looked around the room.

I tried to cover my nervousness at hearing the news of Captain Bligh, the specifics of which I didn't know, by excusing myself to sit in a cane chair. While my back was to the governor, my mind was scurrying to come up with something. Will was sunk against his pillow staring at the ceiling; I'd have no help from him.

"Well, but — we got so little news on the main," I stammered. "And, the story was only briefly told us in those American ports where we were getting our stores before coming here."

Lying was not my nature. I disliked making up any untruth. Yet what could I do? I could only hope that my excuse satisfied him.

Governor Wanjon clasped his hands.

"Well, why should you care what humbug Captain Bligh got himself into? You were nearly extinguished by the sea, but as God would have it, you endured. Did you know, young lady, that you traveled the equal distance of Captain Bligh? I think you should be decorated for this bravery, and when I send your bill to the admiralty, I shall recommend that they decorate you as a formal tribute."

I blushed when he said that and I felt the heat rise under my collar, for I knew not what he meant by his "bill." "What bill do you refer to, sir?"

He coughed delicately into a handkerchief. "I refer to the cost of your quarters, and to the doctors and nurses in your attendance. . . . It costs greatly, my dear. Our little government colony cannot support the likes of such — but your admiralty will take it up without a qualm. They did so for Captain Bligh, and they will certainly do so for you."

Governor Wanjon grinned.

For my part, I was beaten out of my usual measure of speech. Nothing could undo us more swiftly than the admiralty's knowing of our whereabouts. Yet I had to quickly cover my discomfort.

At last, the governor having run out of things to say, excused himself. At our door he asked if I was satisfied with our lodgings. I told him I was fully satisfied of it.

"Is there anything, then, that I can do for you?" he asked with a little bow.

"Well," said I, "there's nothing your kindness hasn't already covered."

"Well, I visited your mates next door, and they all seem to be in pretty fine fettle," Mr. Wanjon remarked.

Our lives from that time forward were nothing but vexation.

And as the weeks went by, we feared every passing shadow and every cloud that covered the sun. Still, all might've gone well had it not been for Emmanuel's fever and Will's loose tongue.

Captured

The next two months slipped by — or, should I say, they stole by — because we were quite unaware of time in this pleasant land of sandalwood and honey. All the same, I spent many hours knotted up with worry whenever Will went out at night. It was hard for me to understand why Will seemed so dedicated to his own destruction, when we had been divinely delivered from disaster not once but many times over. In any event, as soon as he was able, he left the cottage every night and took himself off to some dingy grog shop, where he drank more heavily than before.

One morning while Will slept, James Martin told me about Will's foolishness. The night before he'd gotten into an argument with a man who had more glory in him, and they'd had a fight.

"Will was the perfect fool, Mary," James reported as we took a walk together with Charlotte. The paths all around the cottage were hedged with tropical flowers, and the jasmine was just then in bloom.

"Could you not get him out of there, James?"

He said, very edgy, "No, I couldn't. When Will's at the bottle, he's a beast that knows no bounds."

That beast, thought I, will bring us all down with him . . .

but what was I to do? I couldn't very well tie him up at night. Any criticism from me threw him into a fit of rage. I was wearied of his extreme nature. I knew he was dangerous to us all, but I had no idea how to rein him in.

"What's to be done?" I asked James.

"We must keep on as we are," he said.

I said, "Yes, we shall do that," but I said it without conviction, for I saw that what was coming would come.

And it did — that same night.

It was late when the soldiers knocked at the door. Will was gone as usual to his grog shop.

I got dressed as quickly as possible and answered the knocks, which had been growing in volume. There were two uniformed Dutch soldiers, and a man I'd not met before.

"What is it you want?" I asked. "My children are yet asleep."

"We're sorry to disturb you, Mrs. Bryant," said the one Dutch officer. He seemed very ill at ease.

"I don't know how to say this," he said, "but it seems there's a complaint against your presence."

"Who from?"

"From this gentleman here, Captain Edwards. He's from the wrecked ship *Pandora*."

We stood on the small veranda of the cottage and the

only light was the lantern borne by the second soldier. In the shadows, Mr. Edwards wore an English officer's uniform that was badly soiled. He had the look of a vagabond all about his sea-hardened face. He stepped out of the darkness into the half-light. Thrusting his chin at me, he said, "There's no doubt in my mind."

"You're — absolutely sure?" asked the officer.

Captain Edwards answered, "I couldn't be more sure of anything except the sinking of my vessel."

I looked at his scant red hair and wrinkled skin. He was a sight, all right, and his cold, steady stare cut me to the quick.

The interview completed, the three men backed up. The first officer told me that they should return at sunrise, and I should be ready. All the while, my heart jumped. I took my breath in little secret gasps. As soon as they were gone, I tried to form a plan. But I could think of nothing. Then, moments later, James Martin appeared at the door.

His face was white as a ghost.

"I was listening at the door," he whispered. His lip trembled as he spoke and his green eyes glittered. "We can't leave without Will."

"Help me get the children dressed," I said.

Charlotte cried at being awakened in the darkness, but

she went willingly and limply into her clothes. Emmanuel was hot with fever. He offered no protest other than a sigh.

The night was thick and wet, and the moths beat about our faces. I closed the cottage door for the last time. The other men were waiting outside on the dark, still lawn. Then, without speaking, we all went forth into the unknown night of palms and vines.

All were accounted for except Will and Nat Lilley, whose job it was that day to watch over Will.

We had no torch and wouldn't have used one even if we did. As we entered the bush that lay behind the cottages, the tree frogs chimed and the smell of rotting herbage rose up all around us. It was a mass of withes and soft, mucky ground underfoot.

Charlotte, whose hand was clutched in mine, kept asking, "Where is it we're going?" To which I had no answer, and just said, "We're going."

James, who bore Emmanuel for me, said, "He's all of a sweat, Mary, burning like a lamp, he is."

"Each night he is like that," I answered.

It pained my heart so that I wanted to stop and cry — just break down and cry. Yet if I had, the men would have crumbled like dry bread. They were, to tell the truth, more flighty than I was. In truth, I was frightened only for the sake of my children. For myself, I had no fear. Indeed, it was anger I felt — anger at Will and the world, and the crazy fix we were in.

Once we stopped, and Sam Broom grumbled, "I should've killed the bloke when I had the chance."

"Who, pray tell?" asked William Allen.

In the muggy dark with a mere wink of starlight, I saw Sam's huge sullen face come near mine. "It's her bloody husband that done it," he muttered. "Out every soppin' night and drinkin' — that done it. Drinkin' and braggin' on his great escape from Port Jackson. How he stole the governor's own boat right under his nose, and sailed it himself over three thousand miles to Timor, with his woman and children wailing all the way."

"Is that the way of it, then, Sam? Is that what you heard?" I asked coldly as we pushed through the acres of vines.

"It is, Mary," he answered.

The night drew all around, and the cheeping frogs and grawking birds settled for a moment of stillness upon which we heard the distant barking of dogs and the curses of men.

"They're coming for us, Mary, you can be sure of that," said James Martin. "I think it's best we just surrender. It'll go easier on us, for we don't know what Will's done against us."

I heard the wisdom of that, and I gave in to it. One look at little Emmanuel and anyone would've done the same, I

can assure you. There was something in that face of his . . .
something that spoke of the end of us all.

So we were caught and brought to gaol and thereafter handed
over to Captain Edwards, who'd made those charges against
us. He knew our story. He knew we were the escapees from
Port Jackson. There were handbills and he'd posted them onboard his ship before it sunk in a gale. He knew our faces,
and his accusation sunk deep as an ax after Will had bragged
his loudest at the bar.

My husband, by the way, along with Nat Lilley, was snared
even before we were. There they were as we came in — all
disheveled and ratty — sitting spaces apart, as if they hardly
knew what had happened.

To Governor Wanjon, Captain Edwards gave a grisly report of our stealing a navy vessel, provisions, and arms. He
said we were scum, not fit to live.

"I will take them," he vowed, "to Newgate Prison, where
they shall all be hanged. There'll be no commutation of sentences this time."

The governor shook his head. Dazed, he met my eye.

"I cannot but think there must be some error here," he
murmured, wrinkling his brow. He was pitiful in his distress —
it was all out of his hands, and I could see he was undone by
the charges, and his own helplessness to alter them.

Even now it's hard for me to fathom what a turmoil of events, what a tempest of coincidences, brought on our imprisonment.

Edwards figured largely in it, though. He'd captured the mutineers from Captain Bligh's *Bounty,* and he was commissioned to take them back to England to be hanged. Then his ship was sunk in a storm.

Anyway, now he had the *Bounty* mutineers — as well as us — in his charge, and he was in a great lather of self-importance over it all.

The next thing we knew, we — all but me and the children — were chained and double-locked and thrown into a Dutch prison ship called the *Rembeng.* I was allowed to take care of the children, but I was always accompanied by an armed guard.

Emmanuel worsened. Charlotte got sick again, and soon she refused to eat.

For the sake of my children, I prayed to God for some clemency. But none came. In no time, we were packed off to Batavia; and that was the end of our days in Timor.

Now Will hung his head like a dead man, and he refused my face altogether, and until he fell ill with a fever for the last time, he wouldn't speak to me at all.

November 1791

We arrived in Batavia, that festering seaport.

In a trice, all the good sunshine and fine food of Koupang faded from memory. In Batavia our flesh was devoured by lice, nits, and the other vermin we knew so well from our days on the hulks. The banks of the port were rampant with rats. I watched them as they clambered onto anything floatable. They knew how to scavenge, all right; and they hastened to the ships whenever they came in.

I shuddered at the sight of one rat the size of a cat, who, sailing out to us on a piece of crate, climbed the mooring stay, then the hawser, until it got aboard, where it slinked under some canvas by the hold. We'd meet again, I figured. At night, most likely. For it was necessary to kick like a mule when you felt something on you. Often enough, I awoke with my feet bleeding from rat bites. So as to not waken you, they ate your heels free of skin, one little layer at a time.

Overall, the unwholesomeness of Batavia claimed the lives of almost all who were ill. A marine told me matter-of-factly one day that the entire population of the town was buried about once every five years.

As it was, we heard the floating corpses knock against

the ship in the night — the canals were full of them — rotting bodies that even the fish wouldn't eat.

If we thought we knew hell before Batavia, we were wrong. For we knew only purgatory.

Batavia was hell.

Under these dire circumstances, poor Will and little Emmanuel clung but tenuously to life. They were soon taken to hospital, where I was permitted to nurse them under the watchful eye of an armed guard. My dear husband had thus far overcome the worst of odds, including the hulks, transportation, the starvation colony, a near-fatal flogging, escape in an open boat, and the long fever that came afterward. However, this new fever had him in its clutches, and didn't let go. He babbled inconsequentially most of the time when I mopped his brow, but on one occasion he said, "I rue the day I was born to be man of the sea, and though I have loved Mary Bryant, I rue the day she ever met me. . . . I am the ruin of everyone on this ship. . . . Let no one forgive me my drunken mouth. . . ."

Will spoke of this unknowing he was on a hospital bed but fully aware he was slipping away.

Emmanuel had no fight left in him. I spooned water into his mouth, but his eyes had no light. I feared the worst, for him as well as for my husband. And as for myself, God somehow saved me thus far from the ague, though every one of us had had some little touch of it, or worse.

At night I dreamed I was back on the *Charlotte* with Catherine and Mary Haydon. I woke in tears remembering our love for one another. All of it cursed by a silk bonnet. How I missed their faces now. And wondered . . . were they alive?

December 1791

⛵ On December 1, 1791, my son, Emmanuel Bryant, was consigned to his maker.

On December 22, 1791, my husband, Will Bryant, followed him.

Each was buried in Batavia.

I wished to follow them, but yet I still had my precious Charlotte and my God-given will to live and to hope . . . for life, not death. I clung to this passionately — that God wanted me to live. For what reason I didn't know, but I felt he was saving me for something.

I was witness to more tragic events when we put to sea. It wasn't long, you may be sure, before James Cox, while walking in chains at the lee side of the ship, pitched himself overboard.

That he sank from sight was proof of death to the sleepy marines, who were supposed to be watching him. I thought otherwise. A stronger swimmer there never was, and, you may know — his hands were quite free.

Indeed, he was less than two miles from shore.

I prefer to think that James made it to the green mainland, where he started up a new life, and is there now enjoying it. There is something in me that doesn't accept the indignity of death. Particularly in a man so ill used by society as James Cox.

With my own family on heaven's shore, safe and sound, it wasn't death at all. They parted from my company to go to a better place, was how I saw it then, and how I think of it now.

Poor little Samuel Bird died of fever.

Then there were only the seven of us.

March 1792

The past two months had gone by as woefully as any I could remember. We could take no pleasure in seeing the many coral islets we passed, or anything else, for that matter. Sickness deprived us of everything but our little shred of sanity.

Charlotte's condition — her fever and cough — worsened. I had it myself — everyone did. It wouldn't go away. But it besieged the little ones, and Charlotte was now wracked in misery. Most of the time she slept fitfully, tossing and turning. Her breath came in rattles and starts that were dreadful to hear.

Finally we reached Cape Horn.

And there, got transferred to the HMS *Gorgon*. This ship was under the command of Captain John Parker.

My old friend Watkin Tench had been commissioned to this ship, and it was he who got us onboard the *Gorgon*.

Our desperate hours tween decks were finished — for me, anyway. Captain Parker ordered my release from irons so that I could take better care of Charlotte. When he first laid eyes on me, he exclaimed, "Can no one see that this woman is sick and her daughter so desperately ill?"

Captain Edwards was still our dark, avenging overlord. But, fortunately, he wasn't in command of the *Gorgon* — just the prisoners.

"It's your ship. You can do anything you want, sir," said Edwards sourly. "But I must warn you, these are the most devious criminals ever to escape from Botany Bay."

Captain Parker smiled but said as cold as ice, "I suppose the sick child is also a villain, eh, Mr. Edwards?"

The other ran his stubby fingers through his thinning red hair, and said nothing. Then, stonily, he saluted, and left us.

Captain Parker called after him, "It *is* my ship, and I *will* do as I see fit."

Hearing these words, the tears coursed down my cheeks. It was the first singular bit of kindness I'd seen since Koupang. No doubt, Mr. Tench was a party to this, a friend as always, but he remained as removed as the days of old.

From that day on, Captain Parker's wife was at my side much of the time; she, too, had such a kind heart. Each afternoon she brought Charlotte all kinds of good things to eat. Nor did I ever see her with a cloth over her face to keep the sickness at bay. She got good and close to Charlotte and me, and never once feared for her own safety.

So once again I was hopeful of my child's recovery. Although the terrible truth was that Charlotte hadn't spoken since the death of Emmanuel, I believed she would talk again when she felt all right.

That wasn't to be the case.

May 1792

It got so hot, we could barely breathe. Below the lower gun deck it was insufferable.

Five youngsters — all of them children of marines — had died.

Charlotte held on, but many expired from the heat alone.

One day, some weeks past the Horn, Watkin Tench came over to speak to me. I was standing by the fo'c'sle, giving Charlotte a little taste of sea air.

He was as blue-eyed and good-looking as ever.

"Well, Mary, it's been a while, hasn't it?"

"Indeed, it has."

"I suppose you know nobody blames you for your flight from Botany Bay."

"They don't?"

"Quite the opposite. They think you're a hero."

"A hero who's going straight to the gallows."

He took me by the shoulder. "You can't think that way, Mary. I keep trying to step in, and do something. I have my report to submit, you know. It shall be heard; and I shall step in."

"I fear Death's in line ahead of you."

He shook his head, despairing of this. "You mustn't give up hope, Mary. You've got Charlotte to think of."

"If I think of her now, it's only about losing her. You have to — sooner or later — see things as they are, not as you want them to be. You can't understand how tired I am of all this. How terribly tired . . . even of talking. For it brings little but despair."

That was the last thing I said to him, or he to me.

Charlotte Bryant died on the sixth day of May. It was five years and six months since I was sentenced at Exeter Castle.

Will had been gone for a little more than four months.

Emmanuel, five months.

I felt awash in the great drift. Even my memory was bearing me back to another, kinder time, so that when I woke in the night, I called out for my sister, Dolly.

And, every night, I dreamed of Cornwall.

I saw myself skinning pilchards and picking flowers.

And in my dreams I was the same age as Charlotte.

The age she'll always be.

London Town

July 1792

The end drew nigh.

James Martin, Sam Broom, William Allen, Nat Lilley, William Moreton, and I were all brought to Newgate Prison as soon as the *Gorgon* touched England's shore. From the first we expected ill treatment of the worst kind. I was exceedingly surprised at what awaited us.

As we clanked through the streets, I expected the jeers that had accompanied our carting to Exeter Castle so many years ago. In its stead — and so much to our amazement — we were given not catcalls but shouts of encouragement and noises of praise. We were lifted in spirit even though the gallows road lay just ahead.

In gaol, the conditions were much the better from those we were accustomed to, and our irons were removed. I still bore the scars at waist, wrist, and ankle from the years of transportation.

There is a great freedom of the press now in England. As the years have changed my face, so have they changed the face of politics. The American outcry of Tom Paine — Freedom — is broad upon the streets and sold in newspapers to whosoever should buy.

So we were now portrayed as our country's greatest

escapees, the heroes of the day. Freedom seekers in our own right. In truth, I knew not what I was or even what I might have been had the situation been different.

They called me the "Girl from Botany Bay," as if I hadn't a name.

I was now a single person, a widow, as I might call myself, loosed from any obligation except death. And then came this roly-poly man in great coat and fancy waistcoat, with red-wine-colored cheeks, who claimed to be James Boswell, the great lawyer.

I wanted to believe his sincerity, but I couldn't. It seemed that all hope had just gone out of me.

I saw the shafts of sun that came through the bars of my single cell, but for once I cared little for them. Nor did the fact of my approaching death lay hard upon me.

I hadn't any fear, or any hope. What should one fear who has lost everything? Betimes, I worried that I would lose their faces — Will's, Emmanuel's, and Charlotte's — but I didn't care if I lost my own. In a sense I felt I already had. There was nothing left of me but something to dispose of.

August 1792

Mr. Boswell, plump and flush, began to make regular visits to see me. He came into my cell, cane in hand, one morning, and I asked him point blank, "Why do you walk about like a common man when you could ride in a carriage?"

At this he burst out laughing, and I feared he would choke. Beads of perspiration popped out of his face, which was red as a beet. "I walk because it pleases me, young lady."

"Is that why you visit me, sir?"

He strode about the cell, then came creaking right up to my face and peered into my eyes so that our noses almost touched. I could readily smell the claret.

"I come here, my dear, because it pleases me to think that the magistrate Nicholas Bond will be favorably disposed toward your case once he sees what a brave and righteous woman you are."

"Am I to be so admired?"

He waved off my question with a grin. Then he called for the guard to bring in a huge hamper full of fresh bread, cheese, fruit, and chocolate.

I must confess that this, more than anything else, brought me quickly to my senses. If this man were in fact the Devil, he was tempting me with just desserts. I fell upon the food.

While I ate — for nothing, not even death itself, could stop my pleasure in this — Mr. Boswell explained that Nicholas Bond, the magistrate, was someone he knew. Moreover, he knew the undersecretary of the home office and the Home Secretary with whom he had gone to school.

I doubted none of this. But I reminded him that I was still a woman under capital sentence.

"We're six convicted criminals and we've broken transportation orders. The penalty, in case you didn't know, Mr. Boswell, is death."

He stood still, and his eyes danced. He chuckled, and that great pear-shaped body wiggled. He pointed his well-manicured finger at me and, wagging it, said, "The penalty foreseeing you, Mrs. Bryant, is a free pardon."

"I think you have it wrong, sir. This is England."

Mr. Boswell walked in a tight circle with his hands deeply pocketed. The sweat rolled off his round cheeks.

"When you go before the judge, Mary Bryant, all that I ask of you is that you treat him exactly as you are here treating me, with no deference whatsoever, but also with no disrespect. You are the genuine article that my dear friend Mr. Rousseau writes of in his confessions, and I would sooner go to the gallows myself if it would save a hair on your head. But, merciful gods, that shan't be necessary. If all goes well, I shall be on holiday the day after we get this thing cleared up."

Moments after his black heels clicked away, and I heard him humming off into the distance, I sat in my cell and cried for the first time since the *Gorgon*.

The following morning my eyes were dry, however. It was to the magistrate's office that we went, early in the morning, all five of us to see the honorable Nicholas Bond.

That was a morning for you — the streets as we passed in chains were thronged with people shouting kind words. I heard a man holler, "You won't go down without us, Mary," and another who said, "We're all on your side." Over all, I heard a drone of noise and saw a blur of faces, and above the din, a child sang out, "Look, there's the girl from Botany Bay."

The magistrate's office was packed with spectators.

Nicholas Bond presented himself, white-wigged and dark-coated, and the gaolers brought us forward through the thick hedgerow of arms and elbows, heads and hands.

People patted us on the back. One towheaded girl caught hold of my iron-braceleted hand.

At the back of the crowd, I glimpsed Mr. Boswell. He was too wise to wave but he did tip his hat slightly.

Each one of us in turn was called to the docket. Starting with James Martin and ending with me, we each gave testimony to the horrors of our past lives. We spoke the truth, giv-

ing no extra effects, as it were, but stating that we were cru-
elly treated from prison to prison, from ship to ship, and from
shore to shore.

Upon Sam Broom's confession of — "I wouldn't be here,
strong man that I am, were it not for that little lady there" —
he nodded at me.

Nat Lilley did the same, so did James Martin.

Yet James waxed poetic, adding, "Mary's a saint, Your Lord-
ship. She made our suffering bearable. She steered us, guided
us, and guarded us. Including her poor dead man, Will, and
her two precious infants who never lived to tell their part in this
misery concocted by the home government, Your Honor."

He had the silver tongue, James did, being Irish. And
when he was through talking, the whole place burst out with
loud huzzahs and shouts. Then, quite suddenly, it was over,
and the place drew still as my name was called, and I
stepped up to speak for myself.

The magistrate looked through his spectacled eyes at
me — peered, is more like it — and he said, "Do you, Mary
Bryant, admit to the leading role you played in the escape of
the prisoners, some of whom yet remain alive in this room?"

I told him, "I do, indeed, sir, and would again, if so
forced."

"— would *again,* you said?"

I turned quickly and caught Mr. Boswell's nod.

"That I *would*, sir."

"Pray, why?"

"As we were all dying, not of disease only but of cruelty at the hands of the mariners, and of rotten victuals, and insufferable living conditions, and as many of us were already dead —"

"Already dead?"

"Some dead of flesh, sir, and some dead of spirit, but all, in the main, dead of something, though some looked alive as some do here in this room."

This brought on some jeers, and the magistrate had to pound his gavel for silence.

Lastly, he asked me, softly and clearly, "So, if transported again, Mary Bryant, am I to understand that you would take the terrible chance of fleeing the colony, while risking the life and limb of your family and friends in an open boat; you would do this again, knowing all that you know about that dangerous travail across the seas?"

"I would."

"Why?"

"Because twould be better to die than to live an hour at Botany Bay."

He thanked me, but I — and no one else — could hear him, for there was so much yelling going on. Yet I could read his lips, and I read them well: He said, "Thank you, Mary."

He did not say, as he had before, Mary Bryant, but merely my first name, which I took to be a great, good sign.

And so it was, for when the din died down and the spectators were hushed, we were told by the gaolers that the magistrate had ordered us back to our cells, but there would be a further examination the following Thursday. My heart leaped — and fell — at hearing this. For what it meant I couldn't imagine. Except, my neck seemed a bit farther off from the gallows.

Mr. Boswell was there to greet me when I was returned to gaol.

"I've never seen such public sympathy," he exclaimed. "Why, Mary, you were wonderful."

"You sound as if I were performing in the theater," I replied.

He chuckled. Then said, "I must go to country, Mary, but I trust you will be as forthright in my absence as you always are in my presence. I've no doubt of your safety and your forthcoming freedom. Here, I want you to read the letter I've written to the Home Secretary, Lord Dundas."

I told him, "I cannot read, sir."

He was taken aback. His face fell, "But you speak so richly, I thought . . ."

"Nonetheless."

"Well, then. I'll read the letter aloud. Listen well. . . ."

The letter is thus put down as follows, exactly as he presented it to me that day:

Dear Sir,

I stayed in town a day longer, on purpose, to wait on you at your office yesterday about one o'clock, as your letter to me appointed; and I was there a few minutes before one, but you were not to be seen. The only solatium you can give me for this unpleasant disappointment, is to favour me with two lines directed Penrhyn, Cornwall, informing me that nothing harsh shall be done to the unfortunate adventurers from New South Wales, for whom I interest myself, and whose very extraordinary case surely will not found a precedent. A negative promise from the Secretary of State I hope will not be with-held, especially when you are Secretary, and the request is for compassion.

I always am,

Very faithfully Yours,

James Boswell

After reading it, Mr. Boswell gloated over the sound of the words, but seeing that I took no satisfaction in his wording, he asked me how it sounded. His eyebrows went up, and he had a look of childish anticipation.

"It's pretty words," I avowed.

His eyebrows hitched up a notch. "So?"

"I wonder if so great a man as that, so lordly a lord, I mean to say, has the time for —" Here, I groped for what I might call us.

"Fallen angels."

"Yes, if you say."

"And . . . damned angels, if I do not?"

I nodded.

He laughed and clapped his hands together, and said, "Oh, Mary, how I wish I'd met you sometime earlier in my life —"

"Before my wings were cut?"

He snapped his fingers, and smiled. "I fancy you, Mary. But not in the way you think, perhaps. I am done with romancing young women, if you want to know the truth. But I am not done with truth. You are one so admirable to me that I would spare no expense of labor to set you on your way. I am in love, you might say, with the idea of you, Mary. You are the heroine I always wanted to read about."

I said nothing. What could I reply to such an effusive tongue? Then he told me he had to go, that there was someone waiting for him at a tavern.

"I hope you have a fine holiday," I said as he went through the bars that locked behind him. Mr. Boswell went off in his flapping-greatcoat rush.

"He didn't hear you," the guard called out.

"He hears everything — and nothing," I said. But the guard was gone, and he didn't hear me, either.

Thursday came and went, and with it, not a pardon — but, on further reflection, not a sentence, either. The magistrate interviewed us again, more briefly than before, and then announced that we were not to be sentenced to death; nor would we be freed from Newgate.

We were to remain there until further sentence might be decreed. It was called an "indeterminate sentence."

Meanwhile, the *London Chronicle* carried a story that, we were told, was most favorable to our case. The public clamor raised up, and a collection of food, clothes, money, and water was brought to each of us. We rejoiced in this and wondered what might happen next. The gallows pole seemed farther off, but the bars of iron that held us were no thinner, and we were getting no younger.

A long time passed.

Days, weeks.

I wondered what happened to Mr. Boswell.

Had he forgotten all about us?

Leaves of Tea

One whole year passed by without my seeing very much of Mr. Boswell. During which time he did nothing, he said, but write letters to people of importance, trying to boost my cause.

I grew most discouraged. Some days, I lay on my pallet and slept. Others, I stared through the bars at the jackdaws crowing on the tops of buildings and remembered the days with Will, our little hut by the sea, and my blessed children. It all seemed so impossibly long ago. I myself felt old. Once, seeing my face in a dipper of water, I had a start.

The face looking back at me was surely not my own. There was age in it that had sorely overtaken my once youthful appearance. I now had a countenance that reminded me of my mother's.

Then one day I was summoned from my cell to speak to the magistrate again. Surprisingly, no others were brought along. Just me. I had no idea what the meaning of this was, but I was allowed to walk clear between the two gaolers, as if I were anyone upon the street of a Sunday.

At the magistrate's gate, I was met by Mr. Boswell.

"Glad I am to see you, Mary," he said straightaway. He took off his tall, silk hat and made a little bow.

"Where have you been all these long months, sir?" I asked.

It was not much of a greeting on my part, I confess. I felt put out with him since he earlier had shown such favor to me and then had just gone away. I pined for his company and his good cheer.

"Is my tardiness to be held against me, then?" he questioned.

"I missed you."

"I've been hither and yon — on your behalf," said Mr. Boswell. "I've even raised a little fund for you. You shall see what I've accomplished, dear girl."

At this I felt a little jump of the heart.

He opened the wrought-iron gate. We went up the broad steps and into the magistrate's office, where the musty odor of books and dust pervaded the air. Surprisingly, there was no assemblage there this time. The hall was so empty that our footfalls clattered on the hardwood floor.

Mr. Nicholas Bond was peering over his spectacles from his high wooden chair. Under the brilliance of his white wig he looked no different than when I saw him last. Now he gazed on me, saying nothing.

For a moment, I listened to the great oaken clock that towered beyond Mr. Bond's disorderly desk. It ticked and tocked, and my heart was just ahead of it — but I imagined that each were of the same volume in that awful, stuffy room.

Then the magistrate cleared his throat and, studying a certain paper he held outstretched in his hand, he began, forthwith, to read aloud:

> Whereas Mary Bryant, alias Broad, now a prisoner in Newgate, stands charged with escaping from the persons having legal custody of her before the expiration of the term for which she had been ordered to be transported AND WHEREAS some favorable circumstances have been humbly presented unto us on her behalf, inducing us to extend our Grace and Mercy unto her and to grant her our free pardon for her said crime, OUR Will and Pleasure therefore is that you cause the said Mary Bryant, alias Broad, to be forthwith discharged out of Custody and that she be inserted for her said crime in our first and next general pardon that shall come out for the poor convicts in Newgate without any condition whatsoever, and for so doing this shall be your warrant, GIVEN at our Court of Saint James's the Second Day of May, 1793 in the Thirty-Third year of our reign.
>
> By His Majesty's Command,
> Henry Dundas

All of which fell like music upon my ear — for, though I knew not what all of it spelt, yet I knew the gist of it: I was a free woman at last.

Upon the completion of the reading, Mr. Boswell escorted me out of the office. The two gaolers gave me the heartiest congratulations. Mr. Boswell withheld himself, I thought. But then, as we stepped out on the street, the gaolers went their way off toward Newgate while we, Mr. Boswell and I, tarried some little while in the sun.

I confess I felt a tug in the gaolers' direction. It was as if I couldn't bear to be unburdened this soon.

But there we were . . . there I was . . . on the sunlit cobbles, free as the very breeze that refreshed our faces. And as the carts creaked the stately coaches wheeled by, and all manner of people passed us as they went about their business, I felt myself gathering my strength, so as to face a storm, or a strong coming tide. I clutched Mr. Boswell's greatcoat then, and pinched a little corner of it to steady myself.

"How long has it been, dear girl?" he asked me.

"Seven years and four months," said I.

"Then I suspect you've paid your debt for stealing that hat — or was it a scarf? I can't remember."

"Nor does it matter," said I, "now that I'm free."

"Are you up to seeing the new lodgings I've squared away for you?"

I nodded. Then he took out of his waistcoat pocket a thick brown envelope.

"I marked this 'Mary's money,' you see. It's all I could garner from my rich friends. It should be quite enough to see you through, however."

Of a truth, I was afraid to look at it . . . money, *for me?*

And then we walked, my arm in his, until we came to Little Titchfield Street, where he'd secured lodging for me — and a fine one it was. Indeed, finer than anything I had need of.

Mr. Boswell was very thorough. He did things the whole way or not at all. This was much better than anything I could've imagined — a place to myself. With furnishings!

"So now you know why I was so long in seeing you, my dear," he said as I walked around in amazement. I touched the grand four-poster bed and sat on a tiny corner of it. Mr. Boswell chuckled at seeing me thus; so I asked him what was the matter.

"Well, you see, it *is* your place now, and you can sit a bit more fully on your bed, if you like."

"I will sit how I wish, thank you."

The words came out of my mouth before I could check them. So I quickly apologized to him.

"There's no need to say you're sorry about a thing, Mary,"

he said, and he passed the thick envelope to me, and I
hastily placed it on the bed. The silence seemed awkward
between us. Mr. Boswell gave me a precise little nod and
said, "Well, I believe that should take care of things. I'll have
your box of items brought from Newgate, posthaste. Aside
from that, I took the liberty of buying you some things . . .
clothes and whatnot. Trifles, really. They, too, will be
delivered. Should you need anything, call for me at this
address."

He handed me a white card embossed in fine black ink.
My hands, I noticed, were trembling.

"When will I see you again, sir?"

A playful smile came upon his lips.

"Such good friends must see each other — *often*," he
said. "I shall call on you at least once every few days or so
until you get yourself adjusted."

"What — what am I to do?" I stammered.

He laughed.

"Let's see. Why not visit the Tower of London? St. Paul's
Cathedral. Visit some shops on Little Titchfield Street. Come
and go as you please. You've a life, you know."

"I *don't* know . . . but . . . if you say it is true. The thing is
this, sir . . . for seven years I haven't had one. It's such an
awkward thing for me to say, but —"

"Go on, Mary."

"I know how to . . . survive. But little else."

"Well," he returned, grinning. "Now you'll have to learn to just *be*."

Then he went out laughing into the sunshine of the busy street.

All summer I cherished my newfound freedom. There was time to walk and peek into shops. The parks and streets amazed me as much as the great landmarks of London like St. Paul's Cathedral and the Tower of London, where, as I knew, much suffering had taken place.

I visited James Martin, Nat Lilley, William Allen, Sam Broom, and William Moreton at Newgate every few days. What pain it caused me to pass through that great, forbidding prison door on the other side of which I always felt locked in. Yet I knew that Mr. Boswell was as good as his word: The others were to be freed as well as I. Nor did he ever let up in his inquiries to the government. I brought my friends bread and soup and told them the news of the street. The miners' riots and other such things of interest. London was a-whirling with activity. Events of catastrophic import were of great interest to James. But it was Sam who always asked, "What wars are brewing, Mary?"

"There's fighting in France, Belgium, and the West Indies and — at every remove — people are spilling over with all the news."

"Ah," sighed he, clasping his big hands. "How I long to be in the thick of it."

"You'll have your chance," I told him.

"Who'd have a convict?" he asked. "That is, if I'd be so lucky as to get out."

I told him that Mr. Boswell would secure him a station in the marines — if that was his wont.

"Is there nothing that this Boswell can't do?" pressed William Allen.

Said I, "There's nothing under the sun he can't twirl around his little finger."

Nat's brown eyes filled with tears. "How I'd love to walk in the sun," he said. "Nothing more, just that!"

"And you shall, Nat Lilley."

"I'd settle for a mug of grog with a fellow Irishman," James added.

"Aren't content with the likes of us?" William Moreton queried roughly, elbowing his friend.

"I'm up to my chin in gentlemen of your ilk," James came back, smiling slyly.

"I'll go now and seek the news of your release," I told them.

When I left the poisonous air of Newgate, I always felt a pang of guiltiness. For I left my friends behind and made my way back to Little Titchfield Street, as free as a bird.

That day, Mr. Boswell was waiting at my door. A strange woman was by his side. Drawing near, I saw at once who it was: my sister Dolly! We embraced. We laughed and we cried. Finally, after some minutes of this, we went inside with Mr. Boswell's help, for the two of us might have stayed on the street holding on to each other for the rest of the day.

"Your younger sister came to my door but an hour ago, and so we hastened to your lodging," he said.

I was at once struck by his saying Dolly was my *younger* sister.

"Dolly's my *older* sister," I corrected.

It was then I realized that she *did* look younger. The years of hardship had taken their toll.

"I have news, Mary."

"Our dear parents?"

"Yes, yes. Of course. They're alive, living in Fowey, just where you left them. I've worked myself up to cook in a great house. But the fine news is — an inheritance. We've an uncle who's bequeathed a small fortune."

Mr. Boswell offered a word of caution.

"I wouldn't count on that money until the will's settled. Isn't that right, Dolly? In the meantime, Mary's cared for by an annuity provided by me. Anyway, she's free to go home to Fowey anytime she wants."

There I was, struck by seeing my sister happy as a wren, and hearing that my parents were still alive — I had feared they were not — and then, the very idea of going home a rich woman!

In all this time I'd dreamed of Fowey, night after night. But I was afraid to go home. I feared reproach. Was I going to be scorned? After all, I had been a convicted felon.

I asked Dolly this question, and she replied, "Dear Mary, you are as large a heroine *there* as *here*. You won't cross the street without half a dozen admirers following you. But do come back as soon as you can — we've so much to talk about and to share. Now I must get back to Mrs. Morgan on Charlotte Street where I am the cook. I mustn't be late."

"I promise to come . . . next week."

So she left in a hurry. And I busied myself with plans of departure.

Some nights after this, Mr. Boswell came to Little Titchfield Street in a carriage. I packed my few things, and then he took me to Beal's Wharf, Southwark. There, as he explained, I was to board a vessel and depart for Cornwall. The ship was called the *Anne and Elizabeth,* and the captain was Mr. Job Moyse.

Mr. Boswell and his son James saw to it that my box of things was stowed aboard properly, and that my engagement on the *Anne and Elizabeth* was secure for that night.

We then went to the Boar's Tusk, a tavern on Beal's Wharf. The night was misty and wet, the little fogs clinging to our ankles as we went into the warm tavern. In no time, Mr. Boswell struck up a lively conversation with the innkeeper. James and I followed behind as his father led the way into a glowing kitchen. There we warmed ourselves at the hearth and partook of some lively punch.

Soon after this, Captain Moyse came in and joined us. Well, I must say, we were a loud, happy party.

Much later in the evening and after a fine meal, we found ourselves alone, Mr. Boswell and I. For perhaps the first time since I'd known him, he grew suddenly serious. "Now Mary," he asked. "Are you well taken care of?"

He looked at me over his half-finished glass of grog.

"I must confess, my heart is low — in spite of the pleasure I take in all this."

"I thought as much," he replied.

"I'm so grateful to you, sir — for everything you've done."

He set down his glass and straightened his cuff. "So you're not fretting about money, or some such?"

I felt my heart beat very fast. "Well, you know, Mr. Boswell, there isn't much in this world I'm afraid of."

"*That,* my dear, is an understatement. So, what then is your qualm?"

I hesitated to say. To tell the truth, it was a terrible thing not to be able to sign my name, nor to even be able to scrawl

my initials. Yet I must be able to do so to receive the money
that he was going to send me every six months.

"I can't . . . write . . . to sign for the annuity, I mean."

He smiled, then called the innkeeper over. "Sir," he said,
"kindly bring us a goose quill and some ink. I've paper here
in my pocket."

He unfolded a piece of parchment on which he had scrib-
bled a few random thoughts. When the quill and ink arrived,
he dipped in and made a large M.B. Then he passed the paper to me, saying, "You shall now be able to make more than
your mark, Mary."

My hand trembled as I tried the pen. I could surely have
braved the shark back on New Holland's coast sooner than I
could've done this simple deed. However, Mr. Boswell showed
me how to implant those initials.

"You see, it can be done, without lifting the tip off the
paper."

In no time I was doing all right by myself. And soon it
looked just like his writing. Whereupon he seized my hand
and said, "Now, Mary, you're really a free woman!"

Before I went safely to my ship's cabin, he gave me the
first half of the annuity: five pounds, plus one pound more.

I gave him a little packet of dried, sweet tea leaves from
Botany Bay. I'd kept them all that time. Now I wanted him to

have them, as they were all that I owned, except myself, from that time.

Mr. Boswell looked at them with astonishment. "What are these?" he asked.

"They're the only thing I saved from Botany Bay. They survived all that I went through; they're the sum of my seven years. I want you to have them, to remember me by."

He shook his head in the golden fog of the ship's lanterns. "Mary, you amaze me," he said.

Then he gave my hand a squeeze, and I boarded the *Anne and Elizabeth*. I looked at him fondly from the railing as he walked in that rolling gait of his down the empty wharf and into the shadows of the night. At first light, we began to pull away from Beal's Wharf in the gray gloom. Then we went quietly down the Thames through the fog and out to sea on the way to Fowey.

Epilogue

No more was heard of Mary Bryant after she returned to Fowey. James Boswell continued to send her the annuity that he had promised for another year. She signed her initials, as he had taught her to do in the "publick house," but after November 1794, there is no receipt record with her initials on it. James Boswell died in 1795, and his family promptly canceled the stipend to Mary.

It is probable that Mary grew weary of being famous in her hometown, and she may have moved farther south along the coast. The parish registers of Fowey have no record of her remarriage or burial. However, in the parish of St. Breage, some forty miles southward, there was a record of someone named Mary Bryant. She was married on October 13, 1807, to a Mr. Richard Thomas. This couple had a child, Mary Anne, who was born in 1811. Mary would have been forty-four at the time of the baby's birth.

As for the other participants in Mary Bryant's story, the following facts remain.

Nothing is known of the lives or deaths of Mary Haydon and Catherine Fryer.

Sam Broom was pardoned and he enlisted as a private in the New South Wales Corps. He returned to Botany Bay and was granted twenty-five acres to homestead in the district of Petersham Hill in 1795.

James Martin was pardoned, and his account of the escape was published in the *Dublin Chronicle* in 1792. It is believed that he lived the rest of his life in Ireland.

William Allen, William Moreton, and Nathaniel Lilley were pardoned, but after they were freed, they disappeared into anonymity and there remains no record of their lives.

Watkin Tench wrote several journals that were later published: *Narrative of the Expedition to Botany Bay* (London, 1789); *The Complete Account of the Settlement at Port Jackson in New South Wales* (London, 1793); and *Sydney's First Four Years* (Sydney, 1961). These books are still the complete record of the transportation and settlement years of Australia. Why they are not better known is puzzling.

Tench had a distinguished career as a captain in the West Indies and other colonial outposts. His regret at not staying in touch with Mary doesn't appear in any of his works, but he did write of his personal sorrow at seeing the convicts so mistreated.

Captain Edwards, who transported Mary, her family, and friends from Koupang to England later faced a court-martial in London because of his brutal treatment of the captured *Bounty* mutineers.

The city of Sydney, Australia, was founded by the fami-